FOUR'S
GAME

FOUR'S GAME

JINNIE ALEXIS

Independently published by Kindle Direct Publishing 2023

Paperback ISBN: 9798351633145

Southeastern University Series, #1

The Southeastern University Collection shows the lives of young adults during their university experience. These students are not only working on keeping their GPAs afloat but are also surviving the everyday trials of life. The series embarks on addiction, mental health, sexual exploration, friendship and family burdens, as well as awakening love.

For a better reading experience, the works within this series should not be read as a standalone.

CONTENTS

CHAPTER 1

FOUR

"Four, you did so well tonight," The young woman in my arms bellowed through my ear in a sultry tone, her breath fanning my sideburns lightly while she drunkenly dangled herself on me. As I made my way around in an attempt to dodge reporters, she collided with me. Introductions were brief after getting off the field, but to the eye, the girl was beautiful and fit.

As I looked down at her, I was unsure if she had a few drinks within her system, but she had begun to slur her words a bit. I sighed to myself. After the win tonight for the university, I wanted nothing more than to take a girl to my bed, have a smoking session to relieve my nerves and go to sleep.

Any girl would do. I didn't care, but I hesitated if my pick for tonight was right.

"Yo, Four! Great game, man. We're really making a name for ourselves around here!" The quarterback of the team and one of my close friends, Tremaine Wright, expressed, sticking his hand out to do our signature handshake.

I switched my weight to speak to him. Trey's eyes darted to the woman on my arm, but he said nothing about her, although a questionable eyebrow raised on his face.

As more players were getting off the field, girls circled around us, waiting for us to sign shirts or make plans to celebrate the win for tonight. I wasn't in much of a partying mood. Instead, I wanted to have a few drinks, light up a blunt and then take this broad home with me.

"You killed it out there, bro," I told Trey. He removed his helmet, revealing his honey-colored locs that were damp from sweat.

Our coach was speaking to a reporter with a few of my teammates. One thing I hated the most was the cameras. It was enough that I was well-known around campus and the town, but I hated seeing gossip about myself in newspapers or blogs. Of course, many things were fabricated and dramatized, but other things were true. For example, gossip reports relating to my weekly choices of bedmates were always a topic of discussion, but could you imagine my mother reading a blog about her son smashing random girls week after week? Not to mention the arbitrary relationship promise delusions that consumed many of my university bedmates.

As a man that enjoys lovemaking, I knew to be cautious and protect myself.

"Four, we're hitting the spot tonight. You in?" Another teammate and close friend, Sebastian Hill, said behind me, slapping my head. I already had a severe headache, and this guy would make it worse.

I clenched my teeth with a wince. "No, I was thinking about getting high and crashing with...uh... her," I nodded towards the young girl still in my arms.

Sebastian, mostly known as Bash, gave me a look of dissatisfaction as he looked at the state she was in. "That looks like a real case to me, bro. She looks hammered. Next thing you know, she'll wake up the next morning and claim that you took advantage of her."

"Oh, for Pete's sake, would you choke on a stick and shut the hell up, Sea Bass!" The girl slurred toward Bash, her eyes glistening and her finger unsteady as she tried to point at him.

"The name's Sebastian," He corrected her politely. He gave her another once over and turned to me. "I stand corrected. She probably doesn't even know her own name right now."

"Well, that makes two of us, I guess," I confessed.

"You don't know her name?" Trey chimed in, looking her down as well.

I shrugged. I know what you're thinking. I'm a douchebag, maybe. But at least I am a genuine douchebag. I didn't care to ask for names. When ladies constantly throw themselves at you daily, learning names becomes irrelevant. They were lucky enough for me to remember the night we shared after I got my release.

"You need to get your stuff together, man," Bash continued.

"Not everyone can be a saint in a monogamous relationship like you," I told him.

This fool was damn near married since we began playing together if you asked me. Bash didn't need to have it written on paper that he was legally married; everyone had already assumed it. His girlfriend, Jasmine Wheeler, was his pride and joy. A sweet bookworm that he had met during his first year of university. He tried to hook me up with her friends, but I was too busy having a secret on-and-off fling with her sister, Ada Wheeler.

"I told you I could find someone that can be to you what Jas is to me," He said. "Yet you want..." He looked over to whatever her name was. "Girls like *her*..."

She smirked sheepishly, probably not knowing what Bash had said to her completely, but still rolled her eyes.

I sighed, frowning as I took in her disheveled state.

Maybe he was right, and I should sit this one out tonight.

I believe the young girl was attempting to say more, but instantly her mouth filled up, and a wave of vomit came flowing out in seconds. Being on the field taught me to move fast. I immediately detached her arm from around me and slightly nudged her away. Instead of most of the vomit getting on me, it directly contacted Bash.

He flinched, eyes wide as her vomit coated his uniform and cleats.

Trey couldn't contain his laughter, and once he had begun laughing, other players from our team joined in.

"What the hell y'all got going on here?" One of the players questioned.

Someone else chuckled, "Damn, she really threw up on you, bro!"

"I bet you were tryin' to flirt with her, huh, Bash? So what happened to being married?" Another teammate snickered with Trey as they fell into a circle of laughter around Bash.

The girl stumbled back into a crowd of fans and ultimately fell into some bush. My arm had some vomit on it, and I almost gagged. Warm chunks of her last meal sat perched on my skin, and I quickly shook all that I could get off while wiping the remainder on my uniform.

I must increase my standards on who I will take to bed. This is becoming embarrassing.

"The offer still stands to go to our spot?" I questioned Bash as he looked up at me, disgusted at what was on him.

Luckily, Sebastian was always a good sport and didn't let much get to him. Finally, he sighed and took in a deep breath. "Let's go clean up."

CHAPTER 2

FOUR

"**O**h, come on! That's a load of crap, and you know it." I muttered, running my hand lazily through my ruffled bed hair.

The after-effects of the edibles I'd taken the night before severely weighed down on me. Being high wouldn't have been a problem on any other day, but today was different. My mother decided it was the perfect day to schedule a meeting with the dean of students to discuss my academic progress.

My jaw clenched as she tapped the back of my hand. She hated when I spoke under my breath; it was a strong pet peeve.

"No, what's *a load of crap* is that your father and I provide many resources for your education, yet here you are not taking it seriously, Matteo!" My mother hissed. I shrunk inwardly. It wasn't news that I despised to be called by my name, but I guess that's the blessing of having mothers; they were above many rules.

"Mr. Wittstock, I hate to break it to you; however, your mother is right. It would help if you took your studies seriously this semester, or football won't--" I suspected that this conversation with Dean Dr. Walker would lead to a scolding. Unfortunately, I didn't care enough to listen to the lecture, seeing as my parents have generously funded several events for this university.

"Why are you bringing the game into this?" I interrupted rudely, snarling at him through my hazy gaze.

"Watch it, Four!" My dad snapped. He had been so busy on his latest iPhone that I'd forgotten he was in the room.

"You all pretend as if I don't bust my butt on and off the field for this university! Every practice, every game!" I was tired of them giving me crap for a few failed courses. I will admit that a few of these courses were requirements, but they knew the pressure of the game.

"What is it with you and this childhood attachment to this sport? How can you sit before us with that smug look on your face as you bring shame to this family's name?" My father whined.

I chuckled to him, knowing it would only piss him off further. With tired eyes, I pointed my index finger at him. "My degree is only important to you so you can sign me up for one of your projects a year from now, and I can waste my life away living in your shadow."

My parents were overbearing at times. They wanted to control every aspect of my life.

"Matteo, enough! Don't you dare speak to your father this way! He is right." Finally, my mother spoke, her usual luxurious Manolo Blahnik heels tapping against the polished floors as she paced the room. She ran freshly manicured nails over her recently bleached blonde hair and sighed. "You must take your academics seriously, or you will have to say goodbye to football for good."

Once again, a load of crap! Yet, I bit my tongue. Clenching my jaw tighter than before, I diverted my eyes from them and began tapping my hand on the mid-century leather chair that I lounged on. I was agitated but kept my cool as I knew my parents loved to bluff. There was no way they would give up having a star NFL player as a son at one of the most academically accelerated universities in the state to teach me a lesson. They were wealthy and well-known members of society; upholding their image would always be their number one priority.

"We've hired an on-campus tutor to help you with your studies." My mother carried on.

"What?"

"A tutor, son. You need to bring up your grades, or you will be thrown off the team immediately." Dean Dr. Walker spoke. He sorted through a mini stack of manilla folders on his desk and pulled out a sheet of paper that appeared to have a list on it. "Due to the generous donations Mrs. and Mr. Wittstock have given to Southeastern University, the professors on this list have agreed to an alternative route to save your grades for this semester." He slid the paper to me, but I was already out of my chair, standing defensively.

"What is this? I don't need a tutor, Ma."

"Four, have a seat. We are not through!" My father's voice deepened in hopes of intimidating me.

"Yes, we are," I stated firmly, ready to depart from this amateur intervention.

"Matteo!" My mother called out to me as I began marching to the door.

If they thought I would sit here and listen to them lecture me about grades and my future, they had another thing coming. I huffed, feeling the pent-up agitation building within me, begging for a release.

I really should've brought someone home last night, I thought.

I opened the door in a swift motion, ready to storm out but was brought to a sudden halt as someone stood at the door with her hand positioned up, prepared to knock.

Black square-framed glasses were perched on a freckled button nose while big brown eyes lay behind them. Her body frame was petite in comparison to mine. Her skin was a rich deep complexion with high glowing cheekbones accommodated by full lips. She wore her hair pulled into a bun with tight curls escaping every way.

My eyes shamelessly traveled down the length of her body, and a warm sensation rolled down my spine. Although she wore a T-shirt and regular denim jeans, her clothes couldn't hide her curves.

I don't believe I'd ever seen her before, but she was beautiful.

As my eyes travelled back to hers, I was startled to see her thick brows furrowed in confusion and disdain.

I inwardly chuckled to myself. I guess this girl wasn't fond of my staring.

"Ah, here she is." The dean's voice seemed to pull me from my trance. He was making his way around his desk, standing sharply next to my parents as he lent his hand to our new guest. "Mrs. and Mr. Wittstock, this is Tosha Jackson; she will be your son's new tutor for this semester."

In disbelief, Tosha and I looked at one another and blurted out in unison, "What?"

CHAPTER 3

TOSHA

The frosty air conditioner welcomed my warm skin as I walked into the computer lab. I hadn't been here in a few weeks since I'd been so busy with my other tutoring gigs. I missed this peaceful sanctuary.

"Well, well, I never thought I'd ever see your face around these parts again." Then, I heard the sound of a familiar voice. It was Xan, formally known as Alexander Campbell.

After a lousy spill ruined my old laptop my first year of university, I met Xan during one of my trips to the computer lab. I'd use the computer lab religiously to get my studies done. Then, I embarrassingly put a virus on a desktop by illegally watching a television series. Xan wasn't surprised; he knew that half of the time spent here was for my own personal gain. To my luck, he was well educated in computer tech and was able to successfully remove the virus. I never thought clearing off a virus from a computer would start my childish crush on him.

I smiled once his presence came into my line of vision. This man was a walking dream. He stood behind the rounded reference desk wearing a fitted black long-sleeve top and light-washed jeans hung low around his waist. His muscles were subtle under his clothing, but there was no doubt he was in good shape.

"You know me, I can't stay away from the lab for long," I spoke, digging my hands into my pockets, nervously peering into his mellow eyes.

"The lab? Dang, I was hoping I was the reason why you kept coming back," He joked. The end of his cornrows rested softly on his shoulders while he turned to face me. A warm smile rested upon his face as his eyes met mine.

The soft ceiling light glimmered on Xan's mahogany skin. He had me in a mental chokehold with his neatly braided cornrows, a boyish smile, and a fit body.

"I mean, seeing you is always a bonus," I said, my pitch cracking a little at the end. I cringed; *Get it together, girl.*

Before he could respond, a girl called out his name by the printer station. "Hey, sir! I think the printer is out of ink." She bellowed.

Shifting his gaze to her, then back to me, he spoke. "Duty calls."

"Yeah, no worries," I reassured, watching him walk away while I shamelessly stared at his back muscles and got a perfect look at that tight a–

"Drooling much?" I jumped, ultimately getting caught by an angelic voice.

I turned around swiftly and was able to release the breath I hadn't realized I'd sucked in.

Standing cheerfully next to me was Jasmine Wheeler. Jasmine was one of the students that I was currently tutoring. With other students failing many classes at a time, Jasmine was beyond her level regarding her academics. She wrote papers for other students, could read novels for days, and held up pretty good grades. Aside from her academic accomplishments, she was not accelerating in Calculus II. With mathematics being the main subject I tutored, I was the top recommendation around campus for assistance.

Jasmine was a short-framed girl with dirty blonde hair, rosy cheeks, and pouty lips. Today she wore a white flowy top with a burgundy pencil skirt, showcasing her smooth legs, and strappy sandals graced her feet.

Her goofy smirk caught my attention as her eyes held a playful intent.

I rolled my eyes at her comment. "Can you blame me?" I asked.

She shook her head. "If Bash and I ever split, Xan is definitely my next top pick."

I laughed. "Jokes on you because you and that boy will never separate," I assured her. "And I've already called dibs on Xan, you know."

I've only known Jas for a few months now, but we've gotten close with each tutoring session. I hadn't spent much time with her outside of tutoring because my schedule has been pretty full lately, but whenever we got together for a session, she would vent to me about her days.

Sebastian Hill, or Bash, as we know him, was Jasmine's boyfriend since their first year of university. He was on the football team, and at first glance, the union was a bit questionable, but the more she spoke of their relationship with me, I understood how they found themselves in love.

"So," I began moving to our regular tutoring area, where her things were already laid out on the table. "What's the verdict?" I asked.

She walked with me, diving gingerly into her bag, and snatched out a packet, holding it up with great pleasure to show me the results.

The letter *B* was written on the packet.

"Coming from usually having C's and D's in this subject, this is surprisingly the happiest I've ever been about a silly grade." She raised her hand, and I engaged in the awaiting high five.

"This is really good! You memorized the formulas?"

She nodded. "Not all, but I'm using the flashcard method, and Bash is helping me with practice problems." She sat down, sliding her quiz into her folder.

Opening another folder, she pulled out a yellow flyer and handed it to me. "Here, this is your personal invitation to a party my sister is hosting this Friday night. Her posse and guys from the football team will be attending; you should come."

"Your sister?" I questioned, taking the yellow flyer from her hand.

"Yeah, her dance squad loves to host these parties every now and again." She waved her hands in the air.

"Your sister is a dancer?" I hadn't known that. *Did she share that with me before, and perhaps I wasn't listening?*

Jasmine made a face. "Yeah, surprisingly. She and I are like night and day. You'll see once you meet her."

"I look forward to it." Although Jasmine had shared that she indeed had a sister, I didn't expect her to be on our school's dance squad. Mostly because Jasmine seemed quite reserved.

"There's also a game happening that night. So we can go together if you're available."

"Um...okay." I wasn't sure about going to the party or the game. I've been to a few events before, but it made me anxious being around large crowds.

My iPhone vibrated in my back pocket. Pulling it out, I checked the notification that I had gotten. I had a meeting with the dean of students regarding picking up another student on my roster for tutoring.

"Thank you for inviting me, Jasmine. I'll definitely think about it and get back to you." I assured her. "I've got to go; next week, we're working on the next two chapters. You can read ahead if you'd like."

She nodded to me, and I went on my way.

Many voices erupted from the dean's office as I approached. The dean and I scheduled to meet whenever he had a student in dire need of academic assistance.

My dad and the dean had been great friends throughout high school and continued their friendship even when they chose to follow separate career paths.

Unfortunately, my dad had a few financial hiccups and hadn't been able to cover a portion of my tuition that my scholarship couldn't. However, he was adamant about me continuing my education no matter what. As a result, he was able to pull a few strings with the dean, and in exchange for covering the rest of my tuition and housing, I would tutor students that needed severe academic assistance.

I lifted my hand, balling it into a fist to prepare to knock, but the door flew open to my surprise. There stood a guy probably twice my size. He towered over me with broad shoulders, messy dark curls, and lazy eyes. From his stature, it was evident that he was athletic, but I couldn't recall where I'd seen him before.

I questionably stared at him. His eyes trailed down the length of my body with little to no discretion. His shamelessness stunned me, and when his dark eyes reached back up to mine, I curled my lip at him.

Without missing a beat, Dean Dr. Walker spoke, breaking the silence between us.

"Ah, here she is." He said. He walked around his desk, standing sharply next to a well-dressed older couple. "Mrs. and Mr. Wittstock, this is Tosha Jackson. She will be your son's new tutor for this semester."

That surname seemed to jog back a memory. These were one of Southeastern University's most gracious donors. I knew that I would be starting a new tutoring gig today, but I hadn't known it would be for the son of the infamous Wittstock family.

I was surprised to hear "What?" slip from my lips, but hearing the guy who stood only a few inches away from me join in unison stunned me.

Dean Dr. Walker gestured for me to come inside further, and although it didn't seem like a good idea, my feet moved on their own. The guy also sunk back into the room, allowing me to enter while he kept his eyes fixed on me.

I squinted towards him before my eyes rested back on the dean. "Is there something I'm missing? I've never met any of the parents of the other students I've tutored before."

I scanned his parents discreetly. His father's eyes were glued to the bright screen of his phone while his mother toyed with a sparkling wedding ring on her finger.

Dean Dr. Walker wore a forced smile. "No, no, no, Tosha. Four here is one of Southeastern's star football players." He gestured to the parents. "Mrs. and Mr. Wittstock have donated generously to this institution and brought forth many opportunities. So they were really thrilled that we had a tutor on such short notice as his spot on the field depends highly on his academic performance." This man appeared to be putting on the show of the century.

"As I said before, I do not need a tutor." The guy's voice was raspy.

"Four, you need to take this seriously." His mother said.

"Mother, I don't need a tutor, and I won't give up a spot that I worked years to get." Four–I'm hoping isn't his real name–spat.

I sighed quietly, shifting my weight from one hip to the other.

The father finally took his eyes away from his phone for a moment to join in. "For once, would you stop and think about something other than this ridiculous football fantasy?!" His father's words immediately silenced the entire room. Even I had to take a step back as chills ran down my spine.

I hadn't thought his dad was paying us any mind. Then, with a pointed finger, his dad spoke, "I am spending my hard-earned fortune to put you through this school, with no cost at your own expense, and you, my son, will follow as I say. You will raise your GPA from this point forward, or I will have you suspended from that team immediately!" His father's voice elevated as he scolded his son.

His eyes were fiery as he held his son's gaze in a threatening duel. Four's eyes went down to the finger the father had to his face and back to his father's cold eyes. A smug grin slid on his face as he scoffed, rolling his father's words off his back as if they meant nothing to him.

Without a comment, Four brushed past me, his shoulder grazing mine slightly and he left, purposely slamming the door behind him.

His father sighed. Running his hand through his salt and pepper hair, he muttered to his wife that he would be waiting in the car. He brushed past me as well. I stood in the same spot, my feet planted to the ground, still processing.

His mother, however, took a deep inhale and exhaled slowly. She collected herself and thanked the dean with a warm nod and a touch on the hand. "I apologize for the men, dean. My husband has been on edge with work, and Matteo has a lot of pressure on him. I thank you for your assistance on Matteo's behalf."

She acknowledged me with a sweet smile and grasped my cold hands in her warm ones. "Thank you, sweetie. Tosha, right? He will come around for the needed help; try not to give up on him. You are doing more than you know." Then, with a slight squeeze of my hand, she was out the door.

When everyone left, it was only Dr. Walker and I. He appeared dumbfounded, and I understood the feeling.

"Um...that was unexpected," I spoke nervously. "May I get the semester plan folder?" I asked.

I never enjoyed drama, and being introduced into a situation this way was difficult for me to process. However, since I had a new student on my roster, I needed to create a lesson plan immediately to fit into my schedule. The sooner he passed his course, the sooner I didn't have to deal with his family's theatrics.

CHAPTER 4

TOSHA

The buttered iron skillet sizzled as I carefully flipped my grilled cheese sandwich. My mouth watered as I watched the cheese melt gracefully.

"Girl, what you got cooking up in here?" Niecy, my roommate, spoke as she walked through our apartment door. She'd just come back from her eight a.m. class.

I turned to her while putting the stovetop temperature on a low setting as I knew she would distract me once she smelled my food.

Meet Niecy Coleman. Niecy and I shared the student apartment that Dean Dr. Walker helped house me in. She was going to school for nursing. We were in our junior year of university, and although I had moved in not too long ago, Niecy and I got along great. She was from the south side of Ridgeport, living in the same area in which I resided with my father. All in all, becoming her new roommate was a match made in heaven.

Niecy was about 5'8 with wide hips and a bodacious body. People always assumed we were sisters with the slight similarities we shared, the only difference being that I was shorter and probably a bit chubbier in the face. Although we shared similar physical attributes, we differed majorly in our styles. While I resorted to graphic t-shirts and jeans, Niecy always dressed up. She loved flowy tank tops, patterned rompers, and even dresses.

Today she wore a floral dress with sandals to match. Her hair was styled in neat box braids pulled into a low ponytail. With her bag dangling on her shoulder with books in her hand, a bright smile rested on her face, showcasing her colored braces.

She sniffed the air dramatically, causing me to shake my head at her foolery. "Hmm! Is that cheese I smell?" She asked.

She dropped her bag and books on our sofa, made her way to me, and rested her chin on the crook of my shoulder. "I only see one sandwich; you haven't started grilling mine yet?" She sang into my ear.

I pushed her head off my shoulder and flicked the air.

"You're like an annoying mosquito that won't leave a room," I said to her jokingly.

Reaching for the microwave, I revealed a crisp sandwich with a cup of soup already portioned out for her. She grinned, doing a little dance as she accepted her lunch. "Oh, Tosha, girl, I don't know how I would survive without you in my life."

I laughed at her dance. "Yeah, yeah, I know. Remember this later when you're buying my Christmas gifts at the end of the semester."

"*Gifts?*" She questioned, emphasizing the plural form.

I nodded to her. "Yup, *gifts.*"

She snorted, taking her meal and plopping down on our sofa. "What's this?" She asked.

Glancing over, I saw my bag resting on our coffee table. My bag was open, allowing the yellow flyer that Jasmine gave me to poke through. She kicked her feet up and leaned back with her meal in her lap, taking the booklet in one hand. "The dance squad is having a party on Friday?" She questioned.

I focused my attention back on my grilled cheese. "Yeah, I believe so."

"How'd you get this? You never told me you knew folks from the dance squad."

I took my sandwich off the skillet and plated it. "I don't. Supposedly I know a dancer's sister. She gave me the invite."

Instead of sitting next to Niecy on the sofa, I opted for the bean bag chair adjacent to her.

"Hmm," She eyed the flyer while I stuffed my face with my hot sandwich.

"Well, since you didn't throw it out, you thinkin' about going?"

I swallowed my food, knowing never to speak with a full mouth. "Yeah, if I'm not too backed up with assignments. Jasmine asked me to the game as well."

"I want to go, but I need you as a wingman." She set the flyer down and took a bite. Then, after swallowing her food, she spoke again. "I don't want to be single this semester. I want a little boo thang, plus everyone goes to these games, so it'll be easy pickings."

"Eh, people will be hot and sweaty. You sure this is where you want to meet someone?" I mumbled.

She nodded. "Yup, I need a big, hot, sweaty guy to come my way."

"Ew, girl, I'm trying to enjoy my lunch in peace."

"Uh-uh. Just because your cooter is building cobwebs by the hour doesn't mean mine has to." Her comment, although meant to be a jab, made me laugh. She joined in, knowing that it was comical. "Listen, you can't be stuck on that dude at the lab for the rest of the semester. If he hasn't pulled a move on you yet, on to the next. You already know how guys are."

She was right. Although Xan and I did flirt every now and again, he never made a move to take things further. I thought it was because he was nervous or I wasn't showing more signals that I was into him, but as the weeks continued and semesters passed, sometimes I felt as if maybe he simply wasn't interested. Niecy claims he might not be into women, but it is still unknown.

I shrugged, swirling my spoon around in my soup. "Maybe Xan is just shy."

"Or maybe he likes his salad tossed." I threw a pillow at her. Her head fell back as her shoulders shrugged. "Hey, I know you've probably thought of that reason already; you simply won't admit it."

"Whatever, fool, he's just shy."

"Right." She looked at the flyer again. "Do you have anything in your closet that could put your boobies on display?"

I rolled my eyes at her. "My 'boobies' do not need to be put on display, Niecy."

"And who told you that? Think about it this way, it's in your best interest to flaunt them now while they sit high rather than later when you're sixty-eight, and they begin to sag like an old man's balls."

I almost puked. "Don't you see that we're eating here?" I scowled at her.

However, she didn't care. "Yeah, whatever. But side note, you really did your thing with this soup. What did you put in here? I'm tasting basil, hints of garlic--"

"And my special ingredient, an old man's balls."

"Ah, that's the little twang I'm getting in there. I was wondering what that was." We erupted in laughter, never taking the other person too seriously.

That is what I admired about Niecy the most. There was never a dull moment with her.

◆◆◆

It was Thursday evening. The week flew by quite swiftly. I wrapped up a session earlier with Jasmine and confirmed to her that I would be attending the game and her sister's dance squad party with Niecy.

Although she hadn't met Niecy, she insisted that we carpool. Shortly after, Niecy and I went to the mall to browse for new clothes.

It was time for my first tutoring session with Matteo Wittstock, notoriously known as Four: one of Southeastern University's most well-known football stars.

After the meeting with the dean of students, I did research on my new tutoring student. He went by Four around campus and was a household name for his skills on the field. Off the field, he was recognized as the womanizer who was born with a silver spoon in his mouth.

I took a look at my watch while my eyebrows furrowed. I made sure to send a text with the details of our first session, yet Four was late. I paced back and forth, becoming impatient at the lack of punctuality on his behalf. This was our first session, and it was already off to a bad start.

I rechecked my watch. I planned on leaving if Four didn't arrive in the next ten minutes.

A text came to my phone from Niecy.

22

Can you make General Tso's chicken tonight? I bought soy sauce & ginger.

I texted her back quickly, her text diverting me from my real issue at hand.

Yes, girl! Clean the chicken & prepare a marinade.

She responded seconds later.

Alright, see you soon!

I did a mini food dance as I now had something to look forward to later tonight. As I dug my phone into my back pocket, I caught a glimpse of Four's towering figure galloping across the parking lot, making his way to the local diner. A few university students shouted his name across the lot, causing him to peer up with a glowing smile and a head nod. I couldn't help but take in the sight of his sturdy jaw and crooked smile.

From our last encounter, he seemed drained, but this evening, he appeared revived. The burgundy T-shirt he wore clung to his body like a glove. The muscles in his bicep flexed as he tightened his watch band around his wrist while he approached. His brown eyes caught mine, and he gave me the same intense stare from our last encounter.

I shifted my weight and stood flat on both feet, reaching down to pick up the binder I set on the ground while I waited.

"You're late. You were supposed to be here almost twenty minutes ago." I spoke as Four made it close enough to hear me.

Jogging towards me, he hovered over me. "I didn't mean to keep you waiting. But, unfortunately, Coach killed us today in practice."

As my eyes trailed down the length of his chest and to his midsection, I realized that he was empty-handed. "Um, where are your things? A notebook? A pen?"

Did he think we were meeting to get milkshakes and hang out?

23

He looked at me in confusion. "You have my lesson plan, yes?"

I knitted my brows. "Yes, but the point of this is–"

"Let's go inside. I'm starving." He was doing his own thing, cutting me off and making his way to the diner's entrance. He pulled on the door handle and waited for me to supposedly get with the program.

With great hesitation, I stood frozen in my spot. "Hold on." He prepared to speak, but I stopped him with a finger wave. "I don't know what you think this is or what you think this will be, but let me set the record straight. I'm here to get you a passing grade at the end of the semester, not to hang out with you for fun."

He squinted his brown eyes at me, a strange yet attractive smirk playing at the corner of his lips. Yes, I said attractive. At first glance, I hadn't really studied his features, but now that he was a bit closer, I will admit he was easy on the eyes.

"I didn't think you'd be uptight on our first meeting."

I raised my eyebrows. "Uptight? Well, I hadn't expected you to be this careless for the time of others."

"Careless? Ptch!" He made a face as he rumbled his lips.

I nodded confidently, walking with my binder to my chest and chin up.

Through the diner doors, I went, my mouth still running. "You heard me correctly. We can either do things right or not do anything at all." I paused to him and diverted my attention to the host who greeted us, her eyes lingering on the athlete behind me. "Can we get a booth in the back, somewhere quiet and secluded, please?"

She barely heard a word I said, too busy batting her eyelashes at Four. I kept my head straight, knowing he was burning holes in my back. Do you know when you can feel someone staring at you? This was one of those moments.

She showed us to a table, placing a fresh salt and pepper caddy down along with a syrup caddy. I sat down first, sliding into the booth while lying my binder and bag on the table. Four slid on the opposite side, taking up most of his half of the booth. He placed his forearms on the table, folding his hands, displaying a few rings on his fingers, the watch he was toying with earlier, and a threaded bracelet.

Again, I could feel him watching me. Yet, I ignored it. Instead, I reached into my bag, pulled out a notebook he could use and a few pens, then opened my binder to go over the lesson plan.

"I don't always do the right things." He spoke.

I took a brief look at him, then back at the binder. "What?"

"What you said at the door, 'we can either do things right or not do anything at all.'" I looked up at him again. Still, his gaze was calculating, meticulous in a way. It was as if he had something else he wanted to say to me but didn't. While I stared at him this time, being this close, I could see how handsome he indeed was.

His dark hair fell in every which way as it was damp and messy. Thick eyebrows sat above dark brown eyes with flashy lashes. It didn't hurt that when he did grin or smirk, for that matter, a faint dimple sunk into the left side of his cheek. I wasn't checking him out, simply acknowledging that his parents created a handsome son.

"Something on your mind?" He questioned as he'd caught me examining his features. Then, without waiting for an answer, he grabbed the menu and scanned the options.

I immediately snapped out of it. As embarrassment washed over me, I inwardly decided that I needed to speed up this session as most of my time had already been wasted.

"What are you doing? We need to start now."

Leaning back into the booth, he flipped through the menu casually. "Why? Are you in a rush to leave? There's someone you need to meet?"

I didn't answer the last part. "We've lost enough time already. We need to get as much done until we meet for the next session."

The waiter came to the table, asking if we wanted to start off with anything. He gave her his order, rearranging certain items on the menu to his liking.

"You wanna get anything? I'm buying." He nodded towards me.

I paused for a moment as he held my gaze. "Green tea," I said shortly.

Giving me a once over, the waitress walks away, making an effort to twirl, dip and twist her backside to either get his attention or dislocate her hip. I wasn't sure which of the two I wanted to go with.

"Tea, huh? Not a coffee person?"

"Not particularly." I refocused on the work that needed to be completed.

"We're going to start with these formulas; memorization of these formulas and application are interchangeable. It doesn't matter if you can memorize a formula; you'll be out of luck if you do not know how and when to apply it. The same goes for application; it doesn't matter if you can apply the formulas. If you can't remember which to use for the question, you'll be–"

"Out of luck," He finished off for me.

"Great, you're learning already," I said sarcastically, causing him to crack a smile. "Now, let's get started."

CHAPTER 5

FOUR

She had been rambling for what seemed like ages. Yet, to my surprise, I didn't mind. Of course, I hadn't retained anything she'd said in the last hour, but there was something exceedingly intriguing about watching this woman perform casually in her element.

"Let me see your answers, then we'll wrap up." She said to me, her eyes finally meeting mine again since she went down the rabbit hole of equations and formulas.

I swirled my tongue across my bottom lip. While Tosha was engrossed in completing as much work as we could today, I had been studying her. She was a breath of fresh air from the girls who threw themselves at me. Although she seemed standoffish, I knew it was all an act. I wasn't planning on making any moves on her, but I was confident in my abilities with women.

There was something about her that piqued my curiosity. I had never seen her around campus; Southeastern was a big campus, but I collided with everyone, from parties to games to clubs. You name it, I was there. And I heard of people, as I assumed they did about me.

From my unfamiliarity with her, I assumed she must be someone who blends into the noise.

She pushed the frame of her glasses back on her nose and curled her lip at me as I popped my last fry into my mouth, finishing my meal entirely.

"Did you hear a word I said?" She asked, the sass in her voice undeniable.

I smiled at her tone. "Yeah, I heard you, but you were working too fast. I need you to break it down further for me." I took a sip of my Coke soda.

She scoffed, pointing towards her opened textbook. "Each time I finished a section, I asked if you were still with me."

"That's your version of breaking things down?" I questioned.

Even behind lenses, her brown eyes were intense and challenging. She was just as stunning to me as the day we met in the dean's office.

Regardless of my attraction towards her, I knew to keep my thoughts to myself. She wanted to keep this strictly about teaching and learning.

Sighing deeply, she checked her phone. This wasn't the first time she had taken a glance at it. Throughout our session, she casually took glances at the time. Did she have somewhere to be? Or maybe someone to meet? The question lingered on my mind throughout our session. Most girls around campus would've been throwing themselves at me, yet she was sitting across one of the most well-known athletes, eager to leave. The only logical explanation that came to mind was her having a partner.

I inwardly chuckled. *How sweet; if only Tosha's boyfriend knew who she was sitting across right now.*

"You got somewhere to be?" I spoke.

She looked up at me with innocent soft eyes. "It's just getting late, that's all."

"How about we call it a night and start fresh for the next session?" I suggested.

She nodded, packing up her things and fixing everything in her binder neatly as she once had it. "I've been meaning to ask, why do you prefer to go by Four rather than Matteo, your actual first name?" She questioned quietly after a moment of silence.

"Some things are better left unknown," I stated, the same answer I had given everyone for years.

She hung her bag on her shoulder, standing from the booth. "That's a dry answer." My eyes trailed the length of her body as she stood before me. She was petite, but her body never denied its maturity. The mounds of her chest pressed through her T-shirt, and I couldn't keep my eyes off her curves.

"You realize I can see you, right?" Her voice took me from my trance.

I shook it off. "Lost in thought." I lied.

She raised an eyebrow. "Lost in thought, huh?" I rose out of the booth, leaving money to cover the bill with a great tip. Her eyes followed mine as I leveled my stance. Then, without disconnecting our gaze, she spoke, "Hey, I can't control your eyes but could you at least be discreet?"

I chuckled. Even as I found Tosha's body compelling and she intrigued me, there was no way I would let her know that, especially not this early.

"Don't flatter yourself." I led us to the exit.

I could hear her voice behind me. "Just keep your eyes to my eyes."

I pushed the door, holding it out for her to go through first. She thanked me quickly, now being ahead of me. Then, like second nature, I found myself glancing again, doing just what she was telling me not to.

"Four!" I glanced up. She wore an expression of disapproval on her face. "You just did it again. Unsolicited staring." Shaking her head, she stuck her hand to the sky, and water beads dripped on her finger. She swore under her breath, holding her binder close to her chest.

I looked at her in concern as she got herself situated, stuffing things in her bag and pulling her phone open to check a navigation app.

The rain had taken us both by surprise. I kept my gaze on Tosha, unsure what she was doing on her phone. Then, while the rain fell heavier, a wave of dread washed upon her.

Though, she tried to mask it. "Next session is Monday at 5 p.m. I'll go over everything again with you, okay?"

I nodded. "Where are you heading? Want a lift?" I told her. If she didn't have a car, waiting for the bus would get her soaked in the rain. Also, car services at night were shady, in my opinion. Although I've only known her for a few hours, what good would it make if my tutor got sick from the rain, or worse, kidnapped?

She looked at the app in hand, then at me. I waited as she battled which option would be best for her. Thankfully, the choice of riding with me seemed better than hiking with strangers on the bus and potentially getting sick.

"The gray student apartments just off 32nd Street." She said nervously, unsure about her decision.

"Across the street from Benny's Pizzaria?" I questioned.

"Yeah." Looking into the parking lot as the rain continued to pour, she scratched her head. "You know what? Forget it. It doesn't look too bad. I think I can make it--"

I cut her off. "Relax, you're my tutor. The least I can do is give you a lift home. I'll bring the truck around. Just stay here."

"Are you trying to make up for the fact that you were late and didn't listen to anything I taught today?" She questioned while thunder illuminated the night sky.

"Nah, I'm trying to make up for my unsolicited staring." With emphasis on the word, I mimicked her. Thankfully she sensed my light humor, cracking one of the most genuine smiles I'd witnessed her express all evening. "Sit tight. I'll swing my truck around."

She agreed, and I jogged into the rain.

CHAPTER 6

TOSHA

Southeastern's star athlete was giving me a ride home in the pouring rain after our second encounter. I didn't really know how I felt about him. Mixed emotions, but nothing terrible. Athletes had a reputation across campus. That life came with lots of parties, girls, and popularity. It was a glorified version of high school but on a broader spectrum. Since I wasn't oblivious to that life, I knew to keep my guard up and not let anything, whether big or small, progress into something I would later regret.

Although I didn't want Four to know where I lived, I hadn't checked the weather earlier to know it would rain tonight.

The last transit would come in an hour from reviewing my navigation app, leaving me with two options: get drenched and ruin my hair or take the ride and endure more time with the infamous football player.

Tonight, the football player option didn't seem too bad.

Now I sat in his truck, with the radio on low, playing an old hit from the 90s. My eyes were glued to the window as pellets of rain coated the laminated glass. I slowly traced shapes in the fog to distract me from the awkward silence.

"So what's your deal? I don't recall ever seeing you at any parties or games." I heard him ask.

Keeping my focus on the rain and the road, I answered, "I highly doubt you'd remember every face you've seen at parties or games."

"I'm sure I'd remember a face like yours."

My finger halted from tracing the glass. I wasn't sure if Four was flirting with me or if I was reading too much into it. At the diner, I'd caught his gaze wandering up and down the length of my body, and he did nothing to hide it. This wouldn't be my first experience with a male student who tried to flirt with me during a session, but this was definitely my first time of it being a white boy.

"What high school did you go to?" He brought me out of my thoughts.

"Lakeshore High," I answered. It was a school in the heart of the south side.

"You're from the south side?" I nodded as we came to a red light.

"Hmm, a southside girl that decided to attend Southeastern University?" He kissed his teeth.

I looked at him. "What's so wrong about that?" I asked.

"I didn't say anything was wrong with it; simply rare." He added. "Around campus, it's mostly kids from the east, north, or out of state."

"The wealthy," I stated. "I'm guessing you're either from the east or the north." From the encounter with his parents, I knew Four came from money; there was no denying it.

"My parents are from the north side." Finally, the red light turned green, and it was our turn to go.

"Why'd you say it like that?"

"What?"

"You said your *parents* are from the north side. What about you?" I questioned.

Shrugging, he tightened his grip on the wheel, leaning casually in his seat. "I traveled a little bit everywhere." Then, making a sharp turn, he continued. "I apologize for what you witnessed a few days ago with the dean."

"No need; I know how difficult some parents can be." We were getting closer to my apartment complex finally. I gathered my things to prepare for my departure. It appeared that Four wanted to say more, but he didn't. Still, I could feel his eyes on me again. "You're doing it again."

"Doing what?" He pulled into my apartment complex.

"You're staring again," I interjected. "Make a right, then go straight. It's the first building by the mailboxes," I added.

"If you don't look my way, why do you assume I'm staring at you?"

"Because I can feel it," I said.

He chuckled. "Trust me, you haven't felt anything yet, Tosh."

My eyes shot to his as the truck came to a complete stop. His dark brown eyes were burning into mine with mischief and naughtiness lingering within them. It was something about his eyes that captivated me. One side of me was curious about what Four meant by that statement, but another part felt repelled.

Although this was my third year in university, my dad was strict about me not messing around and dating. He also felt strongly against too much socialization with white folks.

Gladly, Four wasn't my type. Dean Dr. Walker had given me this tutoring position for my benefit, and if I were to continue assisting Four with his studies, I had to set a few boundaries. He had been late for our session tonight, but he also seemed disengaged in the content.

"Listen, I'm not sure what you're thinking will happen here, but I advise you to quickly get those thoughts out of your head." He leaned back, shifting the gear to park, and turned the radio down completely. I continued. "You were careless of my time today, didn't send a text or call to inform me that you would be late--"

"I don't have your number--"

"I'm not finished." I silenced him immediately. "I texted you the location and time of our meeting, so you're lying to say you don't have my number. You have my number; you simply didn't care to save it. Where I'm from, if someone is running you a service, you don't disregard them. I didn't have to wait on you today. I could have left."

"You could have," He agreed.

"Yes, but I didn't. Don't make this harder than it has to be. Show up to the lessons, be courteous of my time, and participate in learning to pass your course." Turning away from him once and for all, I grabbed my things. "Whatever you think is going to happen between us won't. Regardless of what you may believe, everyone isn't a fan of football players. The next session is Monday at 5 p.m. Be there on time and prepared." Opening the door, I said my last words to him. "Thanks for the ride."

Finally, I jumped out, running in the rain to my apartment door to get started on dinner.

◆◆◆

I sighed as I took my hair out of the bun to redo it for the fifth time. Friday night rolled around in no time. I had an early exam which I knew I passed with flying colors, and now it was time to celebrate. The game started at 6 p.m., and Jasmine agreed to carpool with Niecy and me.

I got dressed in fitted jeans, a pastel purple strapless top, and strapped sandals with a chunked heel to give me some height. I accessorized with a necklace and a few bracelets. Reassembling my bun, I pulled it together with my hair tie, slicking it up with gel and a stiff-bristled brush. I twirled the curls on my sides with my finger and made sure to lay any edges that may have coiled up.

"You got any large rubber bands, T?" Niecy burst into my room, holding her braids in a ponytail while she used her free hand to frantically express her words. "I popped my last two hair ties." She sighed heavily, frustrated beyond her boiling point.

I knew the struggle.

"You can have a few of my hair ties," I told her, reaching in my hair box and pulling out the already opened hair ties pack.

A wave of relief hit her as she came eagerly to claim a few. "Thank God, I was about to have a panic attack if I had to wear these damn braids down. I would've been sweating like no tomorrow." She got her hair situated, and I took a look at her outfit.

She wore one of her spaghetti-strapped floral dresses with sandals in which the straps circled all the way up, stopping at her knees. A bracelet on her right arm, a few necklaces around her neck, and subtle studs in her ear. My friend was stunning.

"Girl, look at you," I said to her in amazement.

She twirled twice once she was sure her hair was up securely. "Just a little something I threw together."

I rolled my eyes at her. "Right, you've probably been saving that outfit for a time like this to lure a man."

"Oh honey, these men aren't going to know what hit them once they see me." She looked around my vanity. "Lip gloss?" I handed her a fresh tube that I had just opened. "I was meaning to ask you this. A little birdy told me they saw you and one of the university's most notorious athletes having a little date last night at the diner. Care to share?"

"A birdy?" I looked at her sideways as she pumped out the gloss onto her index finger and applied it to her lips.

"Yeah, can't share the informant's credentials, but that's not important. How did you forget to share that you were on a date with Four, T? You realize that his parents are dripping in money? They even got him his own beach house!"

"Whoa, whoa! Pause for just--"

"Not only did you get invited to this party, but now you're going on dates with athletes? Whew, girl, how are you managing this double life with your studies?" She appeared frantic, trying to get her thoughts in order and place the puzzle pieces together.

"Okay, first, whatever birdy spying on us definitely got the wrong idea, Niecy." I grabbed a bottle of cocoa butter lotion and slathered it on my arms, making sure to get my ashy elbows. "Second, we weren't on a date. I'm tutoring him in a course that he's having trouble in. But did you just say a beach house?"

She bobbed her head. "Yes, girl! I think the party is at the beach house. I heard a few girls talking about it in the lecture hall." She came up to me quickly and flicked my arm.

My brows furrowed. "Ouch, what the--"

"And that's for not telling me about him sooner."

"Okay, well, let me add that he also took me home, and he's not all that."

She paced around my room. "Wow, if we don't have trust within our relationship, what do we have?"

Laughing, I waved her off, rubbing my arm from the tingles of her flick.

"Quit being dramatic. Four is the epitome of a spoiled athlete. Nothing more, nothing less. Had I known the party was to be held at his home, I would've saved Jasmine the gas and declined."

"What?" Niecy asked, hysterical. "Why would you decline?"

"Because last night I had to set him straight. He showed up late, unprepared, and couldn't keep his eyes off my body."

"Listen, I'm a girl that loves her a good manly south-side guy, but there are a few exceptions that I would blindly fall head over heels for. He is definitely top of the list as one of them." She smiled to herself, nodding her head in agreement with her words.

A text from Jasmine came to my phone, letting me know of her arrival. I grabbed Niecy's attention with the wave of my phone. "Ride's here."

Niecy twirled out of my room, leading the way to an eventful evening.

The stadium was packed. A Friday night game at Southeastern University meant any and everyone was coming out to support, watch a good match, and bet their chips on their favorite player. We sat in the student section. On my right stood a group of hardcore Southeastern students, dripped out in more merch than I owned. To my left was a group of guys, making a mess on the bleachers with all types of snacks and drinks that they had purchased at the concession stand. Each guy stuffed their face, roaring with each wave around the crowd.

It was humid, packed, and loud. Finally, the game was winding down, with only a few minutes left on the clock and our scores were surpassing the other team. It was a challenging and intense game. I watched the field closely, enjoying making predictions of throws and catches like I'd been doing since it started.

"'Scuse me, 'scuse me." Niecy's voice came through, and I could see her squeezing past people to get to our seats. Jasmine was close behind with skittles and a corn dog in her hands.

"You wouldn't believe the line we were in to get this," Jas spoke as she sat to the left of me.

Niecy took a seat to my right. She handed me a Reese's as I had requested. "Right, and then these drunk girls tried to skip us." I laughed from the bewilderment written all over Niecy's face as she couldn't believe they really tried to skip her.

Jasmine nodded, opening her pack of skittles and giving a few to Niecy across my lap. "Are we still winning?"

"Yeah, now I see what the hype was all about with this team. The coaches were going at it at one point." I told them, nibbling on my peanut butter snack covered in chocolate.

"I've heard some stories but never seen them play," Jasmine confirmed.

I knew we would win with only a few minutes left on the clock. However, Niecy and Jasmine had missed a large part of the game since they decided to get snacks. But if the game ended soon and we were stuck in the rush of students trying to leave, I don't think I could stomach the chaos.

"You guys wanna make a run for it now, so we're not stuck in the crowds of people trying to leave?"

Jasmine agreed. Meanwhile, Niecy slouched. "We just got back to our seats. I've taken only one bite of my hot dog," She whined.

"Oh, save me the theatrics," I muttered to her, standing from my seat. She eventually gave in and followed suit as we made our way towards the exit, not far enough to hear the time go off and the crowd rave.

It was a celebration for reps, the university, and the players on the field. The crowd went wild, and just as I expected, people were shouting and standing from their seats, and the chaos was about to start. We needed to get moving. Now

CHAPTER 7

FOUR

Another win, as everyone suspected. The season would be good for us, that much I knew. My teammates and I were thrilled, yet my mind was elsewhere. My mood had little to do with the game, even though my right shoulder was in intense pain from a hit I took on the field. Instead, my mind was repeating the events with my tutor the night before.

No woman in this world could deny my charm. However, the act that she showcased last night made me question if she was involved with someone else. I was a confident man who knew my attributes and how women worked. If she knew of my parents and I, why was she so standoffish towards me?

"Aye, man, you better tell Bash that I'm only rolling three blunts, so if he misses out on the rotation, that's on him," Trey said, licking the wrap as he rolled our blunts.

Trey was Southeastern University's most dangerous quarterback's yet to date. He and I had known one another since training together with his previous coach. We clicked instantly from our love for the game. Although we went to different high schools, applying to the same university allowed our brotherhood to strengthen.

I decided to hold the after-party at the beach house after a few girls from the dance squad, Ada included, begged me. I figured since we all were familiar and hung out within similar circles, why not? Trey sat on the couch with a rolling tray in his lap. Drunk college girls swarmed around him, twirling their nails through his honey-colored locs as they whispered and giggled at whatever nonsense he was uttering to them.

The guest capacity was more significant than I anticipated, but I didn't mind. As long as the cops didn't show up and people continued to bring booze, I was going with the flow of things. I searched for Bash among the crowd of moving bodies that filled the space, but the music was too loud for me to focus. Chugging the rest of my beer down, I whipped out my phone.

The first message that came through was from my mom.

Watched the game on television. Congrats, honey! Very proud of you!

It was followed by a kissy emoji and a heart.

I smiled at it, knowing that although she and I both knew how my dad felt about me playing the sport, she was still supportive of whatever made me happy. At times, our relationship was rocky, but she knew how hard it was living with a father like my own. Scanning my contacts, I texted Bash, letting him know what Trey informed me, and went to the kitchen for another beer.

The party was in full effect. Everyone seemed to be enjoying themselves, smiling, drinking, and conversing with one another. Hot girls danced around leisurely. Grinding their bodies as the alcohol took effect on their minds. This was always the perfect way to unwind after a stressful game, this and a post-game ice bath.

I dug into a cooler for another beer. Suddenly, Ada crept up to me with her posse close behind. "I've been looking for you," She spoke, her blonde hair falling around her shoulders in bouncy curls while her eyes flashed flirtatiously to me.

Ada Wheeler was the epitome of a man's dream girl. She was tall and tan with piercing blue eyes that could make any guy fall. Additionally, her beauty also came with talents. She was a part of the dance squad here at Southeastern University.

One sleepless night with her progressed into two, then three, and after our fourth entanglement, I made sure to call it quits. She wanted more than I was willing to give. Unfortunately, our engagements around campus made it hard to stay away from one another. With her being at every game or on the field while I practiced, it was almost as if fate wanted me to finally lock in on one prize and hang up my jersey.

The downfall of it all was that Sebastian's girlfriend, Jasmine, was Ada's older sister. Bash did not know of our involvement with one another. He was very protective of his girlfriend and treated Ada like a little sister. He'd flip if he knew that Ada and I had been messing around. Bash knew the kind of man I was and was aware that I had no plans to settle down.

At least not right now anyway. I was still exploring my options.

Ada and I's involvement was to be kept under the radar. I simply didn't want it to be blown out of proportion. By the watchful looks her posse always gave me around campus, now, I was sure that Ada had been creating a different narrative about us.

Her freshly manicured hand trailed up my chest as she licked her lips. "Good game out there. I saw you got hit pretty bad." Her voice was flirtatious, a soulful nympho at work. She was always good at arousing me with her flirtations.

"Nothing I can't handle." I opened the beer up, chucking the cap in the air. Then, taking another gulp, I twitched slightly as her hands traced my diamond-cut link chain, massaging my shoulders.

"I can take your mind off things, ya know. We haven't really seen much of each other in a while." There was no denying her beauty. With each word she spoke, she caressed the muscles of my biceps gently, luring me into her with each touch. To think I could have this woman down on her knees with her puckered lips around my—

"Man, I've been looking for you!" Trey said, cutting me out of the filthy rabbit hole my mind was sending me to. He popped into the kitchen, sounding winded from his search for me. A lit blunt dangled in his mouth as he handed me a rolled one for myself. "Merk gave us that gas, bro. Don't drink too much. Some guys from the team want to play beer pong and maybe poker in a few, a'ight?"

I nodded towards him, thanking him for his gracious service of rolling up for me.

Trey didn't miss Ada and her lingering crew as a ladies' man himself. "Ladies," He acknowledged, smirking at me subtly as he ducked back into the crowd of drunk bodies.

Ada dug in her purse and pulled out a lighter without missing a beat.

"You're always prepared, huh?" I questioned, allowing her to light my blunt.

She waved her crew off, and with fewer people in the kitchen, she inched closer to me. "I keep essentials with me."

After inhaling, I blew the smoke away from her face. Although Ada appeared to be holier than thou, she'd shown me not to always trust the good girls. Or, more rather, not to trust the girls who portrayed themselves as so. There was always a little

44

mischief in everyone. I inhaled again, watching her trail her hands down the length of my chest and then lower.

I wanted to screw her. Right here on this kitchen island.

Long legs around my waist, manicured nails clawing at my back, and her soft moans filling my ears. I wanted her now.

She pushed our bodies closer. I attempted to pass her the blunt, but she declined. "What I really want is you upstairs with me." She whispered, her voice coming in vibrations to my ears.

The music was blaring, and with a blunt in one hand, and beer in the other, I was ready to risk it all. That is until a moving trio caught my attention in the distance. Through the archway of the kitchen, I could see into the main room, and my jaw almost sunk to the ground as my eyes got sight of a woman I never thought I'd see at one of my parties.

Tosha.

I stepped away from Ada, completely lost in my thoughts. "Four, where are you going?"

What was she doing here? I thought. I had never seen her at one of my parties before. But this party was a bit different. I had allowed Ada to combine her guest lists to celebrate the new girls sworn into her dance squad.

I took another hit and blinked as the smoke almost clouded my eyes from her presence. Yet, there she was, laughing vigorously and mingling with Jasmine and another girl I hadn't recognized. How did my tutor know Jasmine?

My eyes trailed down the length of her petite frame. Her hair was pulled into a tight bun with curls hanging freely on the sides. Regular studs were in her ear while her glasses sat casually on the bridge of her nose. The top she wore was strapless, showcasing the knacks of her collar bones and the smooth richness of her skin. In pairing to this, jeans hugged her hips, revealing the matured curves of her body. She appeared relaxed and mellow, not so uptight and assertive as before.

"Four, what are you looking at?" Ada's voice was like background noise to me. I could hear it, but I was barely paying any mind to it.

My phone vibrated in my pocket. It was a text from Trey.

Come to the din. We started the games.

I gave Ada's shoulder a squeeze, keeping things subtle. "I'll be right back. Trey has a game set up for the guys." I told her, knowing that this wouldn't be our last encounter of the night.

I turned from her, going in the direction where I had seen Tosha standing, but she was no longer there. I kept pushing, knowing that I would surely see her again tonight if I'd seen her once.

◆◆◆

"Chug! Chug! Chug!" People chanted, banging on anything in their reach. Apparently, we had kegs, I don't know who brought them, but after a few games of beer pong, my teammates decided they wanted to clog their bloodstream with more beer. So I stood in the background, observing.

Truth be told, I was too high to interact any further. I'd slowed down on the alcohol as I didn't want to blackout. It happened a few times during my first year of university, and girls took it as an opportunity to take advantage of me.

Now, I made sure to take extra precautions. Trey, on the other hand, could barely stand. He was slurring his words and swaying his body like a tube man. I chuckled as he knocked his hip with some random girl. She was shocked, pushed him off, and mouthed the words "move jerk."

I was ready to call it a night. The house was trashed, and the stench of sweat and booze reeked in the air. I needed some fresh air. I let down my foot as it was posted on the wall behind me and made my way to the double sliding doors leading to the beach pathway. It was a breezy night, cool and crisp, from the aftermath of the previous rainy night.

I enjoyed living in this beach house. It had good memories of my mother, two older brothers, and myself. But unfortunately, my father was always too busy with a project or with his company to join us. So instead, he sent gifts in exchange for his absence. It bothered me then, but I began to care less as I got older.

I inhaled the bracing breeze, my feet sinking into the gritty sand as I walked the path. Groups of intoxicated people stumbled by, congratulating me on the win and shouting good reviews on the party. I saluted them, not wasting much time on further conversation.

The moon was bright tonight. It appeared full, radiant in color, and mesmerizing at the highest point in the sky.

"Four! Hey, Four!" I spun around at my name being called, surprised to see Bash in his swimming trunks. He was jogging in my direction, and as I looked closer, I could see that his beloved girlfriend, Jasmine, Tosha, and their friend were all close behind. "Dude, you smoked what Merk gave us?" His eyes were bloodshot red.

I chuckled at him. "Bro, open your eyes. You look as high as a kite."

He pretended to left hook me, moving with awful coordination, making me laugh even more as I dodged him. "I could say the same thing about you. Looks like you're out here wishing upon a star."

Jasmine smiled at me once she saw who Bash had met up with. "Hey Four, I haven't seen you all night. Let me introduce you to my friends." She called both Tosha and her other friend over. Once Tosha saw me, she stood frozen in place. Her eyes seemed darker under the moonlight.

I stuck my hand out to their friend that I hadn't met. "Four," I spoke.

Their friend resembled a model. She wore her hair up in a ponytail, exposing the sculptures of her high cheekbones. While Tosha and Jasmine were short and petite, this girl was tall and fit. She shook my hand heedlessly, smirking as I rubbed my thumb against the pad of her smooth skin. "I'm Niecy."

Tosha didn't introduce herself to me. Instead, she whipped out her phone and excused herself before anyone could notice it as if she were taking a call. I may have been fried, but I know what a phone screen looks like if you're really on a call.

Though, Jasmine hadn't noticed. She was too busy trying to get Bash's attention while he screamed rambunctiously on the beach, sending punches to his chest in imitation of a modern-day Tarzan.

Niecy signaled me. "Where's your bathroom? I need to freshen up."

"Up the stairs, second door to your right," I instructed her.

She smiled at me, whispering her thank you. Then, as she walked past Tosha, she pushed her in my direction, and they quickly went back and forth, whispering to one another incoherently until Tosha finally gave in with a pout and her nose in the air.

I smirked as I watched them. *Ah, Niecy was setting her up.* I mentally thanked her.

Turning my gaze back to the night sky, I waited for her to speak. After a few minutes of standing, I could hear her inching closer until she was set in the vacant spot next to me. Finally, she let out a sigh. "Congrats on the win."

"Thanks," I said.

"You've been smoking? You smell like you've been smoking." She sniffed.

"A little," I replied, folding my arms.

"I thought athletes weren't supposed to do that."

"We're not supposed to do many things, but we still do."

Another wave of silence washed over us. I wouldn't say it was complete silence, not with the waves crashing powerfully in the ocean, Bash bothering Jasmine in the distance, and a plethora of drunk bodies dragging themselves from my house to the beach and vice versa. Sighing again, she stood before me, her head back to stare up at me. I took down my arms, not wanting to come off as threatening.

"Alright. I wanted to let you know that I apologize for my rashness last night, although some things deserved to be said."

"Is that your best version of an apology?"

Her eyebrows furrowed, another pout taking over her expression. "If you weren't so unprofessional from the start, none of that would have had to unfold."

"Unprofessional?" I chuckled. She couldn't be serious. "Oh, come on. Would you take a moment and come down off your high horse?" I spat back at her.

"Excuse me?"

"Listen," I tried to level with her because one hand had gone to her hips, and I knew that stance was never a good sign. "You are way too uptight. You need to loosen up a bit, Tosh."

"I am not uptight!"

"And defensive too," I added as if she hadn't uttered a word.

"You think you know me, but you don't. You assume your charm will work on me as if I am one of your regular hoochies. Need I remind you that I am your tutor."

"I was trying to get us comfortable with one another."

"Why?"

"You want us to work together and be strict about the books all the time?"

She looked at me, stuck, my words not sitting well with her. I shook my head; she was blowing my high. "You know what? Forget it. Forget I ever said anything." I turned to walk away, but she stepped in my way.

"Okay, wait. Let's stop for a moment. I don't know if it's the liquor talking or what, but I didn't intend to come to this party and start an argument with you. I didn't even know you were the host."

"But you still came."

She nodded. "I found out later that this was your place when I was already dressed and ready."

"You wouldn't have come if I invited you personally?"

"Truthfully, maybe not." She turned, kicking sand under her feet. "I'm apologizing for my harshness in the car. You did a good deed by offering me a ride, and I didn't mean to come off rude."

I watched her closely, twirling her body as she spoke, diverting eye contact as she didn't want to come off small before me. It was adorable to see a different side to her, and it increased my interest in knowing more.

"I apologize as well for making you uncomfortable with the staring. I will try my best to be more discreet."

Her laugh ringed in the night, flooding my ears with its melody. She looked back at me, shaking her head. "You ruined the moment."

I shrugged, not caring. I was glad to see Tosha smiling. A beautiful smile it was. I wanted to spend more time with her. Not just for tonight but maybe over the weekend. It was clear that she did not want to be involved with me as many other girls did. Still, as she was my tutor, we could at least become comfortable around one another to allow our sessions to run smoothly.

"I was thinking," I said, timid about my proposition. "maybe we could have our study sessions here."

"Here?" She looked at me with hesitation.

"Yeah, I live here. I extended rooms to Trey and Bash, but they're rarely ever here." I looked up to find Sebastian and Jasmine, but they had disappeared. "Bash is usually with Jasmine, and Trey comes and goes. The internet connection is great, and it's quiet."

She stepped aside, looking at the house and then to the beach. She was analyzing her environment, trying to figure out her next move. I enjoyed seeing that look. It allowed me to know that she was careful, constantly weighing the options and potential outcomes in her head before doing anything.

"I'm not too sure about that...but I will think about it over the weekend and get back to you."

"That's fair."

"I'm going to search for Niecy. I hope she didn't get lost or start wandering in your place." She stood with her hands folded in front of her pelvis.

"I saved your number, by the way. Made sure to add a few peach emojis to make it stand out." I rubbed my hands together, smirking at the thought that popped into my head.

She kissed her teeth and rolled her eyes at my comment. Although she didn't take me serious, it still produced a smile. "Like I said, I'm going to search for Niecy. Goodnight, Four."

I gave her a comforting nod. "Goodnight, Tosh."

She departed from me with another gentle smile, making her way back to my house, her hips swaying with each step.

CHAPTER 8

TOSHA

The party at Four's was more than I thought it would be. I had never been around that much booze in my life. And that's coming from a girl with a father who drank more beer than Homer Simpson. I had a few drinks but didn't smoke anything offered to me. You never know what kind of crazy things could be slipped within a rolled joint. I was glad that we had gone to the party with Jasmine. She made sure to keep us in the loop with everyone around us since this wasn't quite our scene. She and Niecy also hit it off, better than I had anticipated.

We left earlier than expected as Niecy wasn't feeling too well. I think it was her time of the month. I knew mine was coming soon from the lovely syncing powers of mother nature.

Jasmine didn't get a chance to introduce us to her sister. She said she was in a bad mood. I didn't mind, as I didn't want any negative energy around me while trying to unwind and let loose.

A text was sent to my phone. It was Four.

Have you decided yet?

I looked at the text for a while. The weekend was almost up, yet I didn't have an answer for Four.

"Why are you making that face? Pops giving you hell again?" Niecy asked, reaching over to get the acetone. She unscrewed the top, poured it into a small glass dish, and used a cotton swab to dip it into the translucent purple liquid.

I shook my head. Niecy was one of the few people who knew about my home life. We bonded by sharing stories of living on the south side when I first moved in. She learned of my dad being a sheriff, my mom's passing, and my younger sister struggling to live alone with Pops.

That reminds me, I need to give her a call. It's been a minute since we spoke.

"No, it's not him," I put my phone down, thinking about what to do with my current situation. "It's about my tutoring gig. I usually have meet-up spots designated to certain students."

"And?" She dragged.

I shook my head, reaching for a different color polish. "And now one of my students wants to change the location."

She removed any mistakes she had made on her toes with her damp cotton swab. "Change the location where?"

"His house."

Now she looked up at me, tilting her head to the side. "Wait," She paused, trying to connect as many dots as possible. "Four invited you to his house?"

"Who said anything about it being Four?"

"Girl, lie to somebody else, not me. I can see it all over your face." She gesticulated her hands to appear as if she was swatting flies. "You got that text, and your face hardened." Then, she went back to fixing her mistakes with her cotton swabs.

"The other night at the party, we kind of had a talk. Afterward, he suggested we have our study session at his house. But you know how these athletes get down around campus. So I don't ever want to get mixed up in that crossfire."

Girls around campus held athletes to the standard of gods. They threw themselves at them, hoping and waiting for a moment to be alone with any athletic player they could get their hands on. But, on the other hand, I wanted to stay away from that life altogether. Unfortunately, it came with too many complications.

"Yeah, we all know how the football players get down, but I saw a little spark between you two at the party." She smirked.

"Niecy, please. The swirl life is for you only. My Pops is old-fashioned. I can't bring home no man not cut from our cloth."

"Oh, save me your dramatic daddy issues. You are a grown woman, clear of making your own decisions."

I scoffed at her. "Well, I don't like Four."

"Never said you did."

"Then what are you trying to say?"

She put the cotton swab in a napkin and gave me her undivided attention. "Listen, ever since we've lived together, you barely ever talk about guys or want to go on dates. We don't know what team Xan is playing for, yet you're stuck on him." I tried to cut her off, but she continued. "Your dad isn't going to be around all the time to dictate your entire life. College is your escape; live a little. Hang out with the kid. Not saying go have babies and become a housewife, just saying that this is your life. There are no rules. We went to that party and didn't see Four until the night's end, and what was he doing? Just chilling by himself, minding his own business. You mind your own business. See, y'all already got things in common." She joked. "But seriously, T. It doesn't hurt to sometimes explore and see what comes out of it. Y'all could probably be really cool friends. You never know."

She was right. I knew deep down in my gut that she was right.

Maybe I had built this wall from the parenting of my strict father. He'd insisted that the only way I could ever be successful was to go to university and get a career with my degree. When I was younger, I hated it and even resented him for it. But as I got older, I started to understand why he pushed education as much as he did. If I wasn't glued to the books as hard as I was, I wouldn't have been accepted into Southeastern University. If I hadn't been a tutor, I wouldn't have been able to get this housing accommodation.

With hard work came rewards. Unfortunately, I never rewarded myself or took time off to unwind and enjoy. What would the outcome be if I inserted myself into Four's life or, more rather, allowed him to insert himself into mine?

"Your advice was a bit misleading at first, but I understand," I told her, picking up my phone and shooting him a quick text, confirming my decision.

"Yeah, yeah. I should definitely minor in psych or social work, don't you think?" She pondered to herself, seeming to be in her own world.

A few minutes passed, and then a text came through from Four.

I will pick you up after practice.

Another one quickly followed after.

I promise I will not be late this time.

"KC hasn't answered any of my texts lately. Is she alright?" I asked Pops, shuffling around my room to find the other pair of my black converses. I checked my closet, waiting for my dad to respond.

My dad had called as he periodically always did. Usually, our conversations were always short and cut to the point. He asked about my studies and would remind me to stay away from boys.

Kayla Carina, widely known as KC, was my younger sister. After mom passed, it had been my responsibility as an older sister to guide her, as Pops didn't know how to raise daughters. KC kept to herself mostly, but unlike me, she rebelled against our dad.

"I would hope she hadn't. I confiscated her phone." He said confidently.

Bending down to my knees, I checked under my bed. "What? Why would you do that?"

"Don't you dare question me, Tosha." He said sternly. "A fat C showed up on her interim a few days ago. Seems to me that she's scrolling on these social media apps way more than focusing on her studies."

My shoe was nowhere to be found. "Dad, she's not in grade school anymore. I don't think it's wise that she goes around without a way to contact you."

He kissed his teeth. "KC has a pay-by-the-minute phone in case of emergencies."

There was no getting through to this man.

"Can you at least text me her TracFone number so I can talk to her?" I said, getting up from the ground and returning to my closet. Giving up searching for my black converse, I grabbed my cocaine white Air Forces instead and put my phone on speaker while putting on the shoes.

"Yeah, but don't go giving her any ideas. That little girl has a lip on her." He told me.

I mentally prepared myself for his mess whenever he called. Then, like the good daughter he wanted me to be, I played my role. "I gotta go, Pops. A couple students from my class are meeting together for a study session, can't be late," I lied effortlessly.

I knew he would be happy to hear it, though. "Good, stay vigorous in your studies and away from these no good boys, 'cause boys don't lead to nothing but--"

"Babies." I finished for him.

"Right." He confirmed. "I love you, sweetheart."

"Love you, too. Bye." And with a click, we ended our call.

My phone vibrated, a text popping up from Four, letting me know he was here. I exhaled softly, biting my bottom lip. Here goes nothing.

CHAPTER 9

TOSHA

Four arrived on time as he promised he would. During our car ride to his beach house, I learned that he enjoyed listening to old-school music and could also play the piano. I used to play the clarinet in church when I was younger but didn't have a strong desire to continue as I progressed into my teens.

Four excused himself to answer a phone call when we arrived at his beach house. I got myself situated in his common living space. I wasn't sure what news he received over the phone, but his mood had changed when he returned.

He came down with damp curls, casual house clothes, and a decently rolled blunt hung from his mouth.

Yet, regardless of his disheveled appearance, he came prepared. He carried a pack of pencils and a few pens in hand, a notebook, worksheets of formulas, and scrap paper. He didn't make eye contact with me, simply laid his items on the coffee table, lit his blunt, and waited for me to start.

I didn't mind him smoking around me, granted this was his house, and I was a guest. So I began teaching as I pleased. He quietly listened, doing practice problems independently, graphing, and using the formulas when needed. Not a snarky comment was uttered, nor any weird gaze my way.

It made me feel a little uneasy with him being this quiet.

"How'd you get this answer?" I asked, looking at the worksheet and the answer key. Something wasn't adding up.

He tossed his roach into the ashtray, gazing at the worksheet before his attention diverted to his vibrating phone. The words 'Mom' flashed on the screen. Sighing, he grabbed his phone off the coffee table and excused himself to step out into the hall. I watched him walk away, but he didn't go far as I could still hear him.

"Hello?" He answered. I didn't mean to eavesdrop, but it was hard to block out the sound with him being so close. He sighed to his mother. "I really don't want to go to that dinner, Ma. Can you lie for me? Say I have a game, or I'm feeling unwell?" He whined. "I don't have anyone special to bring, mother. Why is Gramps so hellbent on me bringing a date? Because Keith is bringing Suzie? What does that have to do with me?" He groaned and went silent for a few seconds.

A text was sent to my phone. It was the number my dad had given me for KC's TracFone. I had texted it earlier, letting her know it was me and that I wanted to make sure she was okay. But, as the phone wasn't the easiest to text with, her response was short.

Call U later.

I texted her back quickly, not wanting to miss the opportunity to talk to my little sis. It's been a while. As I tucked my phone back into my bag, Four walked into the living space, checking his watch for the time.

"Um, do you have somewhere to be?" I asked.

"Can we just..." He looked around, his eyes wandering. Then, finally, his eyes traveled to the patio and the beach where the sun was setting on the horizon. "You mind if we take a quick break?" He appeared stressed. The call with his mother must've done a number on him.

"You're gonna smoke?" I asked.

He nodded, coming around to grab the ashtray. The front door clicked as he did so, and his friends' voices came bustling in. "Crap," He muttered. He was beyond frustrated at this point. "Let's go outside before they blow my high." He spoke, and I listened.

I hated to further frustrate people when they were almost at their breaking point. So I grabbed my bag, leaving the rest of the sheets and forms on the coffee table. I followed Four, and we headed out to the beach, where the beautiful sunset welcomed us with open arms.

CHAPTER 10

FOUR

The start of my day was rough. I received a call from my father earlier and purposefully ignored it. However, I knew why he was calling. It was about that time that Gramps liked to have his annual family dinner. It was a family dinner from hell. Gramps was the holder of the Wittstock name, working hard and building a legacy for himself to be passed down. My grandfather took what little he had and made it into something of his own. My father followed in his footsteps, not having much of a choice.

I tried my entire life to escape it. It worked for me, well, up until now. My father constantly reminded me that football was just a distraction and the family business was where my real spot in the world was to be held. We never bonded. We never spoke of anything other than building and designing properties. While that was his destiny, it wasn't mine.

When my father couldn't reach me, he sent the next best thing. Keith, my elder brother. I also ignored his call. The call with my mother really put the icing on the cake for me. I needed a moment to breathe.

I'm glad that Tosha agreed when I asked for a break. The view on the beach was spectacular. This was probably the best thing about the house. It was serene and peaceful. The beach house always allowed me to clear my mind. That's what I needed right now. Stop all of the chaos for once and get a moment to think.

We sat on a large beach towel, not too far from the rustling waves. While I rolled up, we sat in silence, deep in thought.

"You smoke?" She'd been quiet next to me for a period while I'd started smoking. She was fixated on the sea, but after I spoke, she turned to me, her eyes squinting behind the frames of her glasses. I lent the blunt to her, testing her to see if she'd decline or accept.

To my surprise, she reached out to grab the blunt and took a few hits. I chuckled to myself. "You alright?" She questioned after exhaling and blowing out the smoke away from me.

"You've never told me you smoked," I told her honestly. Tosha was a mystery to me.

She passed it back to me. "I actually don't smoke but I did my fair share of things in high school; no one is a saint."

I inhaled, enjoying the feeling of the smoke clouding my lungs. "I never would've guessed."

She shrugged. "Don't get me wrong, I'm not a stoner. I've been taught all of my life that smoking doesn't please God. But a few hits won't hurt *me*."

As the blunt touched my lips, I took a moment to study her. Her index finger rubbed against the pads of her thumbs as she gently rocked her head to the rhythm of the oceanic tune. Her side profile was breathtaking. Her jawline was soft, and her mahogany skin glistened under the warm hues of the sunset.

Wow, she is beautiful. I watched as she licked her lips slowly, oblivious to my staring. I wanted to stick my thumb out and trace it over her plump lips to feel the moisture beneath my skin. There was something about her that was so innocent yet sensual. Images came to my head of my name coming out of those sweet lips while I curiously learned every crevice of her body.

As I fell into a hole of subconscious lust, I could feel my body reacting to those thoughts. Immediately, I shifted my gaze away from the sight of Tosha. I desired to have her under me, riled up and begging to please her. But she'd made it clear that she wanted to keep things strictly about the books. So I needed to sit back and play along. She would soon come to me.

She leaned back on her arms, locking her elbows firm for support. "Would you say that this session was better for you? I know I can teach a bit faster than necessary at times."

"Oh, you realized?" I joked.

She flicked me off. "Whatever, and to think I was feeling sorry for you."

"Sorry for me?" I passed the blunt back to her.

She leaned back on one of her arms, taking her glasses off for a quick moment to wipe her eyes, then took the blunt. "Yeah, you were quiet during the session."

"All work, no play, right?"

She stared at me for a moment before inhaling. Then, after a few more deep inhales and exhales, she passed the blunt back to me. "You are right. All work, no play."

I smirked to myself. Tosha knew the right moments when to push and the moments when to not. She never asked too much of anything in regards to my personal life. If Ada were sitting next to me, she would have been down my neck right now about what was wrong or what she could do to make it better. She would've been begging me to talk to her, questioning why I hadn't returned her calls in days or kept things from her.

Tosha didn't care about anything that pertained to me or my life. In fact, I believe the fact that she was aware of who I was may have seemed to repulse her. Being in the presence of a well-known football player around campus didn't seem like a badge of honor to Tosha. And I liked it. Screw that; I loved it. For once, I felt normal. I didn't feel the weight of the team on my shoulders. I didn't feel my father's judgmental gaze over my head. I didn't feel like the superstar athlete working his way to becoming the next NFL draft pick.

It allowed me to breathe, knowing that someone wasn't trying to pry into my life or get my approval to be accepted into my lifestyle.

"Would you come to dinner with me?" The question had left my mouth before I firmly had time to process and think about it.

She turned to me quickly. Her eyebrows knitted together. "What?"

"Would you come to dinner with me? Formally?" I repeated, taking the clip from her.

She appeared frozen. "Are you...what is this? Are you asking me out? Because I'm not going on a date with you. I'm your tutor and--"

"No, no." I shushed her. "Not a date. It's a family dinner. Every year my grandfather holds a family dinner. He's been doing it since I was a freshman in high school. Of course, it's chaotic, but he desperately wants to keep it as a tradition since we stopped our weekly Sunday dinners long ago."

"I don't think that'll be a good idea. Your parents seem very...high class, and well, I'm not." Then, turning to me, she pushed her glasses back, adjusting them on her face. "I'm sorry,

Four, but it's enough that I have to tutor you, but you really want me to be around your family?"

I frowned. *Oh, here we go.* "Tosha cut the crap." I tossed the roach in the sand. "You once asked why I don't go by my name, and now you will get a chance to see."

"But why invite me? There's plenty of girls that you could take to this dinner to meet your family."

"And here I am asking you."

"Yeah, I don't know why you're doing that, but you can find a better option that can mix well with your family." She threw at me, standing from the towel. She dusted off the sand from her clothes.

"Tosh,"

"No." She patted her knees down. "Find someone else. I'm not getting mixed up in your family drama."

"This is exactly why I need you to come with me. Any other girl would've jumped to the idea if I sprung it on them like this. You're smart, rational, and don't care about my life. It would be my treat to you. Delicious cuisine, expensive wine, and a great show." I needed to get her to this dinner with me. The more she resisted, the more it showed how good a candidate she would be for it.

She picked up her bag, searching through it. "Not a chance, Four."

"Are you serious?"

"Are you?" She threw back. She couldn't find whatever she was looking for, her eyebrows furrowing in confusion as she searched, pocket to pocket.

"What are you looking for?"

"My phone, I can't find it." She frowned. "I think it must've slipped out of my bag and fell in your house,"

I smirked. *Sometimes you have to put your faith in God and sit back and watch Him work.* "Good. Come to dinner with me, or I will keep your phone."

"Have you lost your mind?" She looked up at me as I stood up, my smirk stretching to a full smile while I watched her expression falter.

This was my leverage over her.

"Four, stop playing around. I'm thirsty, it's getting late, and I need my phone."

I nodded. "Awesome. Come to dinner with me, and we can go inside. I will get you a water bottle, get your phone, and take you home before your bedtime."

"And if I don't agree?"

"Have fun trying to catch the bus back home without your navigation app, all while being parched." I grabbed the beach towel and began walking back to the house, knowing that if she was as bright as I knew she was, she would pick the right option.

"You're a douchebag!"

"I've been told!" I threw back at her over my shoulder.

Tosha was coming to this dinner with me whether she liked it or not. She seemed to be the only girl that I could tolerate even while she agitated me simultaneously. And if she was there, I'd have someone to focus on rather than my siblings arguing or my father going back and forth with Gramps. Tosha was my lucky golden ticket. She simply didn't know it yet.

CHAPTER 11

FOUR

"If you missed me that much, you should've told me to come over sooner," Ada purred into my ear.

I leaned back onto my headboard, placing the joint in between my lips and lighting it. I know what you're probably thinking. What am I doing? I asked myself the same question once I invited Ada over an hour ago. Two things I knew needed to end were my smoking addiction and the fling with Ada.

Despite that, the stress of not hearing back from Tosha throughout the weekend positioned me to seek outside pleasures of distractions. I was sick to my stomach at the strange tingles that would build up at just the thought of her.

I trained harder than usual for the next few days, hoping to distract my mind further. However, those thoughts came racing back when I stepped off the field. Tosha wouldn't leave my head. I was losing it.

I did not love the girl or want to be with her.

Anything I felt was purely from my lustful desires.

I wanted to show her the real power I had. The real reason why girls went crazy over me. I wanted to show her that, like every other girl, I could have her also.

But it wasn't that simple with her. I could see that she was meticulous. She would make me work for it or think that I actually would.

I shook my head. *Stop thinking about her, Four. Get a grip on yourself.*

"Four?"

I forgot Ada was here. "Yeah?" I answered lazily. I felt terrible for using Ada like this, but sometimes girls do this to themselves. She knew what the deal was. She already knew of my name and reputation. She desperately wanted to get involved with me, while I wanted nothing more than sex from her.

"We never really get a chance to talk, ya know?" Then, throwing a glance her way, she lay in my bed like a model posing for a photoshoot.

The girl was stunning. No one could deny her beauty.

She licked her lips, running her hands through her blonde hair as she sighed. "There's a concert happening downtown this weekend, and I want to go."

I exhaled my smoke into the air. "You should go," I didn't understand the point of small talk. Tosha never made small talk.

Ada made a face. "I want to go but not alone. Do you want to come with me?" She trailed a perfectly manicured finger down my bicep.

I shook my head at her. Saturday was my family dinner, and I would see my Nana on Sunday. "I won't be available this weekend. I have a busy schedule."

She frowned as I passed her the joint. Taking a puff, she rolled her eyes. "I don't want to come off as if I'm chasing you,

Four, but I think if we're going to be doing this, we could at least hang out more." She said.

Here it comes.

"Not right now, Ada. I have a lot on my plate."

"Seriously, Four?" She sat up, the sheets fell off, exposing her upper body. As she exhaled, she spoke. "So you can invite me over and have sex with me but don't have time to hang out this weekend?"

As I've stated, I wouldn't say I liked smashing a girl more than twice. They become clingy and automatically assume that you want them as a person. Unfortunately, it wasn't the case. Ada was beautiful, but she wasn't it for me. I was not interested in furthering anything with her. Or anyone else, for that matter. As I said, I have too much on my plate.

"I didn't force you to come over, Ada."

She placed the joint on the ashtray and clapped her hands together, probably trying to get my attention. But I was trying to smoke, not deal with this nonsense. While she began her rant, I picked the joint back up, searching the bed for the lighter to get it lit.

"Come on, Four? You're not going to pay attention to me right now?" She threw her hands up in disbelief, and her breasts bounced. I couldn't help my eyes from being zeroed in on them.

Fantasies of our private life began to fill my mind.

"Oh, trust me, I'm paying very *much* attention to you right now," I said to her, emphasizing my words. With her blond hair spread around her shoulders, her face flushed with color, and her upper body out on display, she had my undivided attention.

"Four, I know we've only hooked up a few times, but I want us to hang out without the sex."

"But the sex is the best part." I was being truthful. I didn't want a relationship with her. My plan centered on football. Anything separate from football was a distraction.

She sighed loudly in frustration. "You're being a prick right now." Am I not always a prick?

I shook her words off. "Listen, maybe we can do something next weekend, but this weekend is off-limits, Ada." I didn't want to shoot her down because the sex was good, and whenever I needed her, she did come for me. But that didn't mean I wanted anything further with her. But she didn't have to know that. I needed to keep her in my good graces and play the game of being interested until I got the girl I wanted.

I grabbed her waist, pulling her thin body onto my lap. Even with pouty lips and a mood, she came to me submissively. Wrapping her arms around my neck, she pouted, looking me in the eyes with her bright blue ones. "You're thinking about this too hard. Just relax, and once I'm not so busy, I'll make time out for you." I lied. "Alright?"

Staring into my eyes, I knew she was wondering if I was being sincere. I wasn't. But she seemed to buy it as she nodded, cozying her naked body closer as she leaned in and pushed her lips onto mine.

Let round two begin.

CHAPTER 12

TOSHA

I was dreading today. I tried to talk Four out of this last night, but he didn't want to hear it. His mind was set and refused any other proposition I tried to offer. I told Niecy about the dinner. To my surprise, she was enthused and intrigued that he invited me as his plus one. Niecy said things get real once a girl is introduced to the family. Well, I ain't want nothing to get real over here. *Let it be fake, and let's keep it that way.*

Nonetheless, Niecy insisted that I look my best around those folks as they would talk behind my back and run my name through the mud if I didn't look the part. I didn't care what they said about me, behind my back or face. I was going to this dinner, but my vessel was void.

Niecy took on the role of painting my face with makeup and styling my curls, so they sat beautifully on my shoulder.

Since I didn't have the money to purchase a top-notch expensive designer dress, I wore an old dress I'd bought for a previous family event. It was a black body-con dress with a sweetheart neckline and short sleeves. Unfortunately, since I gained a few pounds in college, the dress was a size or two too small. Still, with the help of Niecy and the Instagram illusion of sucking in the tummy, I was able to get the dress zipped up and practiced my breathing to ensure it allowed for perfect oxygen intake.

With my curls hanging to my shoulders, a light layer of makeup on my face, and this dress hugging my body, I looked stunning. I only wished I had dressed up this nice for someone like Xan rather than Four.

Speaking of Xan, a day ago, I ran into him at a local bookstore. We spoke briefly, and he asked me to get coffee with him sometime. I wasn't sure what to make of it, but I agreed. We exchanged numbers before he had to run off to make it back to the computer lab. Although Niecy had her doubts about him, my crush still lingered.

Four had arrived to pick me up for the eventful family dinner. I must admit. He looked dapper in a long gray trench coat, a black shirt underneath, and fitted black pants. Rings decorated his thick fingers, while a thin chain was tucked under his shirt and suede leather Chelsea boots covered his feet. I could sneak in a few looks here and there while he drove.

We drove in silence for most of the ride, the radio being the only sound among us. It was a comfortable silence. We both seemed to be on a roller coaster of thoughts. I had jitters as to what I was getting myself into.

"Matteo is finally here, sir." The guard at the gate spoke into his headpiece, allowing us access to enter the matte black steel gates of Four's grandfather's estate.

My mouth hung low, bewilderment washing over me as my eyes grew in size at the reality I was currently facing. If you were to tell me a year ago that I would be driving in a sleek truck with one of the university's most valued players and pulling up to a mansion to have dinner with his family, I would have laughed. I was experiencing it first hand, yet I was still bewildered.

As Four rolled the window back up, he ran a hand over his face, trying to collect his thoughts.

"Is there anything I should know before we go in?" I asked him.

"No." He said shortly, his tone rigid.

"That's it then? No warnings? No rules or things you wouldn't like me to say?" I pushed. He was dragging me into the lion's den with him, yet I had no blueprint of how this operation was going down.

As he pulled the car up the driveway of the beautiful estate, young men stood outside, ready to attend to our doors the moment Four put the car in park.

One man pulled my door open, which caused Four to raise a hand to him. "Charles, I don't like the valet service Gramps loves dearly. Shut her door. I will take care of it."

My door was shut again with no further question. Four waved off the other man who came to his side. Then he turned to me. "I didn't insist on you being here with me to condition you with a role to play as my date. I brought you here for the complete opposite of that. There are no rules. I simply want you to see a side of my life that I rarely ever show to anyone. My family is a handful behind the glitz and glamour displayed to the public. I think this will help us get to know one another better." He fixed his stylish shirt and ran a hand through his tamed hair.

"Okay," I said to him as I unbuckled my seatbelt.

He gestured towards the glove compartment. "Could you pass me a bottle of cologne? Any will do."

Opening up the glove compartment, I found a little black Bible, a few napkins, and three designer colognes. I chose the round bottle, passing it over to him and watching as he gave himself a few sprays. The aroma of his cologne filled my nostrils, and a soft tingle ran through my body.

Exalting himself seemed to send my body into a frenzy. I shook my head to jolt my mind from any unwanted arising thoughts.

Thankfully, he was on the move. He jumped out of the car and opened my door for me. With an outstretched hand, he stood with his back straight, his eyes only focused on me while mine wandered in every way. I took hold of his hand and allowed him to help me down. I didn't miss the grip he briefly had on my waist or the freshness of his new smell that filled my nasal tract as the wind blew graciously.

I'm not sure what it was, but seeing him dressed up like tonight rather than in his everyday garb significantly affected me.

"It's a pleasure for you to finally grace us with your company, honey." A sweet, melodious voice which I've heard before spoke.

Four shut the door to his truck, allowing the valet men to drive his vehicle off the driveway, away from our vision. A genuine smile stretched on his face as he took in the sight of his mother.

The woman was stunning. She appeared well polished and vibrant with a light layer of makeup on her face and her hair styled in a 1940s pin-up hair-do. With bleached blonde hair and cherry red lips, she favored Marilyn Monroe. Her attire fit her look. A floral knee-length dress with ankle strap stiletto heels and gold jewelry to pull everything together.

Mrs. Wittstock stood in the doorway, with a smile tugging on her lips as she looked at her son, but confusion washed over her face when he stepped aside and revealed me. She tried to mask it, but her expression of dubiety was hard to hide.

Four stepped to her, and she wrapped him in her embrace. "I'm glad to see you too, Ma." He spoke tenderly to her.

I remember seeing her in the dean's office. She appeared more nurturing and understanding of Four, contrasting with how his father spoke to him.

She sniffed him, unabashed. "You smell delightful, Matteo." She said with a subtle tone before her gaze landed on me. "I see you've brought a guest."

It almost made me laugh to see how she was behaving. During our session at his house, she called him to ensure he attended and brought a guest. Maybe she simply wasn't expecting that guest to be me. However, she reached out to embrace me. Skeptical of it, the hug was awkward on my end. I didn't mean it to be; it just was. "I remember you. You're Matteo's tutor, correct?"

I nodded, but Four spoke. "Her name is Tosha, Ma."

She smiled at me, her red lips bright and warm. "It's a pleasure to have you joining us tonight. I hope Four's not too much of a handful to deal with."

"If anything, she's the handful that I have to deal with." Four muttered under his breath.

I elbowed him in the stomach. It was like a reflex. I didn't mean to do it, especially in front of his mom, but his snarky comments needed to have some type of consequence behind them.

"Ow! Mother, I promise she's not this abusive all the time." He clenched his stomach in pain, and his mother's expression blossomed into a smile between us, a little twinkle in her eye as she watched me sneer at him.

Turning from him, she extended her hand to me and gestured to follow her. "Enough of the theatrics, Matteo. Dinner is almost ready, and the festivities must begin. Shall we?" I took her arm, still skeptical about where her stance was in the family but decided that if Four was comfortable with her enough to feel this at ease, I would simply have to piggyback off his actions.

"Four, this is disgusting," I whispered to him, forcing myself to slurp down the grilled-up oysters he coerced me to taste. This was my third hors d'oeuvre he had coached me to try, and my faith in him to be my guide had diminished completely. He seemed to take pleasure in my suffering, unable to hold in his laughter whenever I tried something and it didn't fit my liking.

I cannot stand this man.

Upon entering the beautiful mansion, Mrs. Wittstock gave me a brief overview of the estate. Next, we traveled to the dining hall, the living space, and a few powder rooms nearby in case I needed to freshen up. During this time, Four stayed close behind us, as no one had come up to us to make acquaintance yet.

Mrs. Wittstock held my hand tightly, her hospitality on full display as she showed me famous paintings, wall art, and the indoor elevator. I was thoroughly engaged while she rambled. It allowed my mind to ease up on Four and obtain a distraction.

Nevertheless, he stayed close behind us, shadowing us as we walked. His mother didn't mind that he was close behind but spoke little to no words. She seemed used to him always being this close to her and away from the other family. Finally, the short tour ended as one of their domestic workers allowed Mrs. Wittstock to know that the first course would be given soon and that Gramps wanted everyone in the dining hall.

Now listen. When I heard of the dining hall, I thought of a bigger version of a dining room. You know? Something simple. I don't know if sometimes I think these ridiculous thoughts or if I actually believe them, but I was deeply mistaken.

In little words, the dining hall could be described as mystical. Classic colonial-style paintings decorated the walls while a gigantic chandelier hung from the ceiling. There was a massive table at the center of the room while a mixologist worked in the corner. Three musicians played live music, and waiters worked the room with hors d'oeuvres, champagne, and wine.

I took a few glances at everyone to be aware of my surroundings but didn't hold anyone's gaze for too long. I received a few stares, most of them in secret. Four was oblivious to this and tugged me to a neatly set long table. He pulled me in every way, persuading me to try things I never knew people could conjure up. Unfortunately, the food served did not sit well with my taste buds. I tried ceviche de camaron, Snapper Crudo with a sauce on it, and now I was slurping down oysters. He really owes me for this one.

He was smiling so hard that lines were forming around the corners of his eyes. "I know." He spoke, watching me as I took a sip of the glass of water he had given me. "Have you ever tried escargot before?"

I paused. "Snail?"

He nodded. "Snail but made elegantly."

I falsified my barfing for dramatic effect. "I'm already nauseous just thinking about it."

He smirked. "I mean, you've come this far; why stop now?"

"Because I might throw all of this up before touching the main dinner." Then it hit me. "Oh my gosh." I turned to him. "Will the main dish taste this nasty as well?"

The laughter of Four was cut short by a voice interrupting our conversation. "You know Gramps takes pride in his starter course, Four."

The voice was stern, filled with authority and prestige. I turned robotically, needing to see who was speaking to us.

Before us was a huge man, as large as Four, with a clean shaved face and dark hair gelled back. His eyes were deep forest green, bringing out the accents of the suit which he wore. A few jewelry pieces resided on his neck and wrist but what caught my attention was the thick ring on his right hand.

It wasn't a wedding ring, but it had the initials KW imprinted.

"Keith." Four spoke, staring at him but not taking a step to embrace him.

"Four." He spoke back, then his eyes went to me. He gazed at me, licking his lips as his eyes shamelessly trailed my body.

Four swatted his hands in his face as if he were a fly. "Where is your sense of respect?"

He ignored Four. "Brother, why must you always be so defensive? I was merely appreciating your date tonight." He reached his hand to me, taking mine in his. He raised it up, tapped his lips lightly on my flesh, and gazed deeply into my eyes.

Today would be the day that I learn all of the undiscovered truths of Four, after all.

"May I ask your name?" He spoke politely.

I could feel Four blowing out steam from his nose like a bull at a rodeo to the side of me.

Still, I answered Keith, pulling my hand from his touch. "Tosha," I said.

He didn't seem phased by my action. Instead, he appeared smugger.

"Keith. What a pleasure to meet you."

"Likewise." My answer was short. The interaction seemed strange, and I didn't know how to maneuver around them. If he had Four this worked up next to me, I knew something far more significant than me was going on between them.

"Darling, how could you leave me alone with Gramps knowing the man could talk for centuries?" A seductive voice came cruising into the conversation, and it was a woman who favored a modern-day Snow White.

Her face was pale beyond measure, hair dark like a raven, and lips painted softly with a stain of red. Her nails were black, long, and sharp. A red dress hugged her body while she wore stiletto heels similar to Mrs. Wittstock.

She greeted Four warmly, with a kiss on the cheek and a squeeze to the chest, but when it came to me, instead of acknowledging me, she tried to pass me her glass as if I were one of the wait staff.

"This wine was God awful. Go and fetch me something tart, a fresh red plum or cranberry will suffice. Quickly." The woman snapped with her other hand in my face.

Four's facial expression twisted up at the woman's act, and he gently nudged her empty glass back to her, almost tilting it out of her hand. She appeared distressed at his action but got her clarity once he spoke.

"Suzie, I know the fake contacts you wear may blind your vision from time to time, but I will help you see clearer. Just because you were once a worker in this estate a few years ago doesn't mean the woman standing next to me is also one." He spat fearlessly.

Miss Suzie, shocked at his words, turned to Keith, which I'm assuming is her *darling*.

"Four, it was a foolish mistake. That is all. No need to bring up the past. Suzie must've gotten her mixed up with the other staff." Keith said, defending his woman.

What the heck do these folks got going on here?

"I don't care if she was mistaken, drunk, or delirious. I've been with Tosha all night. I'm sure Suzie can look at her and see that she isn't dressed as one of our wait staff." Four's words rolled off his tongue with spite.

Seeing how riled up Four had gotten from Suzie's action, Keith stepped in on her behalf. Speaking to me directly, he said. "I apologize for my fiancée's rudeness."

I knew he was only apologizing to be polite and there was no real sincerity in his tone.

I replied back accordingly, matching his tone. "No worries, you can't help it that you chose to be with a woman raised in a barn," I looked at her, my eyes glancing from her head to her toes. "Or potentially, a cage for that matter." I tugged on Four's arm, feeling like he was the only secure person I had in the room. "Let's try more hors d'oeuvres, shall we?" I said sweetly, pulling him away and leaving the couple to wrestle with their own thoughts. At that moment, I knew that this was only the beginning of a crazy night that was to come.

CHAPTER 13

TOSHA

After trying more starters, Four took me around to meet other members of his family. First, I learned that Four's grandfather had adopted his cousin, Vincent, who preferred to be called Vinny. Next, I met Gramps and his very *youthful* girlfriend. Their age gap was definitely an elephant in the room, but no one pointed it out.

We all sat at the long dining table with its sumptuous plate setting, embellished fruit bowls, and glasses of wine and champagne all in reach for us. There were various slices of bread and spreads at our disposal. The staff set our first course down in front of us, which was some sort of soup. The portion was outstandingly small. I looked around to see if anyone else was confused, but everyone seemed as if this was their norm.

I reached for a slice of bread, and of course, Ms. Snow White thought it would be the perfect time to open her mouth again to me.

"Oh, honey, lay off the carbs. Instead, you should work on losing as much as you possibly can right now. Men prefer slim and fit women."

"Susana!" Mrs. Wittstock interrupted as she overheard what Suzie said to me.

I looked at Four, and he raised an eyebrow at me, questioning my next move. I smiled sweetly to his mother as I took my slice of bread anyway and set it on my side plate. "It's okay, Mrs. Wittstock." I turned to the camouflaging dwarf. "Unlike you, Suzie, my men enjoy having some meat to grab on instead of trying to wrestle with bones all day. As I suppose Keith does every night with you."

Four started laughing next to me and his cousin Vinny joined in. I could even see Keith trying to hold in his laugh as his fiancée shot daggers into my skull.

Gramps stood from his seat at the end of the table and tapped his glass with a spoon. "Settle down, my loved ones. Don't let a little bread and butter scare you, Susana. My darling, you look a bit flushed. Eat to your heart's desires."

She guzzled down her red wine, still looking my way in disgust and loathing. *Come on, girl. I know exactly how to handle you*, I thought.

"So there is a guy in your life?" Four questioned me softly. His voice fanned against my ear and sent ripples down my spine. I straightened my back up immediately. No way was I going to let his presence start affecting me now. I know what could be and what could not be. And from what I could see now, I knew Four and I were from two different worlds. A different world that I did not want to be a part of.

I turned to him after chowing down my piece of bread. "Why are you asking?" I questioned.

He shrugged, licking his lips as he leaned closer to my face. "Nothing, just curious. I wanna know if all of your needs are thoroughly being met." He spoke softly to me as Gramps gave a speech to which we both weren't paying attention.

I looked in his warm brown eyes, the smell of his cologne still emitting the freshness it once had thirty minutes ago. "What needs do you speak of?"

Smirking, he said, "You tell me." and leaned back into his seat, turning his gaze to Gramps, who was going on and on about something I had completely blurred out.

Instead, I found myself staring intensely into the side profile of this man in who I've suddenly found a deep interest. It wasn't as if I wanted to run off into the sunset with him holding hands and singing hymns until we saw the stars; no, that simply didn't fit into my real life. Instead, it was an interest in peeling back the layers which would allow me to know him. I sighed to myself. This went against everything I stood for.

I made sure to never get romantically involved with any students I tutored. My father also raised me to never be in the position to ever get caught with a white boy. He informed KC and I that they came with generational baggage that many would never try to unlearn.

Although I knew Four and I would never be a thing, I couldn't deny my physical attraction to him. However, being around his family so intimately made me feel like I was being invited into something I wasn't ready to take on.

The invitation tonight to be his plus one alone made me uneasy. Yet, something seemed different about him. He seemed light around me this evening. He remained close and didn't stray too far from me to leave his sight.

He trailed behind when his mother pulled me aside to acquaint me with his father. I'm not sure if he was hovering intentionally for his sake or mine. His father said a few words to me as his eyes were glued to his phone, consumed with work, I assumed.

Mrs. Wittstock seemed bothered by it, but she didn't share her disdain publicly. Instead, she excused herself from us, and we later met Vinny.

Vinny seemed more of a brother to Four than Keith did. They both shared their love for football. However, although Vinny played the sport, he was still following his family's path by joining the family company. On the other hand, Four has completely turned away from the idea.

I didn't blame him. His heart wasn't in it. Can't blame a man for not wanting to do something he isn't passionate about.

"Did you useless rats start this family dinner without me?" A loud voice took me out of my mental trance.

The entire room got quiet as our eyes followed where the voice had come from. In walked a tall man. He was thinner, but he shared similar features as Four and Keith. His hair fell wildly to his shoulders while rings and tattoos covered his hands and arms.

As he made his way to us, cigarette fumes and weed stench took over the room.

"You've got to be kidding me." Four's father mumbled under his breath. It was the first complete sentence I'd heard him say all night.

In contrast, Four's mother pushed her seat back, getting up to embrace him.

"The real show has just begun." Four whispered to me.

Suzie had taken her wine to the head, emptying her glass completely with one big gulp. In frustration, Keith ran his hand over his face while Gramps sat down, shock taking over his demeanor.

"Who is he?" I whispered back to Four.

"My middle brother, Matty, aka the problem child." He took a sip of his water. "Dad is going to lose it. You want more water?" He asked me, unmoved by the situation at hand. I looked at him with a raised brow, and he shrugged. "Suit yourself," He mumbled.

Mrs. Wittstock welcomed her son to the table, getting him a seat between Suzie and herself. Matty cheesed to everyone but began to speak directly to his father, who was trying his best to divert his eyes completely from Matty.

"What's up, father? You don't look too happy to see me?" Matty chuckled as he waved for the staff to pour him a glass of wine.

Mr. Wittstock looked at his son in disbelief as he spoke with a stern voice. "Matthew, you recently got out of rehab for your last DUI. You should not be here right now. You should be in remission."

"*Remission*." He mocked his father, saying the word with an ignorant tone. "Fill it up, baby." He spoke to the staff who was fixing his drink. She did as he said, setting it down to him. He didn't allow the glass to firmly touch the table before he guzzled it down, drinking it all in one sitting and then instructing her to fill it up again.

"Matty, honey, take it easy," Suzie spoke to him, uncomfortable to be next to him.

He waved her off. "You should worry more about starving yourself than my intimacy with this wine." He grinned devilishly. "I heard last time you passed out, my big brother had to drag you to the car, leaving an important business deal on the table." He shot at her.

Shocked, Suzie turned to Keith, pointing her manicured finger in his face. "Keith! We agreed to never tell anyone about that!" She screeched.

He shook his head. "Baby, that was a huge business deal of mine!" He fired back.

"We are almost to be wed. In sickness and in health, Keith! In sickness and in health!" She slammed her napkin down on the table. "If you tell your family every detail about our private life, maybe this engagement was a mistake!" She pushed her seat out and stormed out of the dining hall.

Matty was guzzling his wine as he smirked at his brother.

Keith shook his head at him. "Really, Matty?" He slammed his napkin down as well and stood up from the table. "And you wonder why Gramps didn't care to invite you here. I'm not sure which one he hates the most, between your drug addiction, alcoholism, or taking it up the backside. But for me, none of those things ever mattered. Your constant need to stir up the pot will ruin our relationship!" Keith stormed off, his anger igniting from his body like steam.

Matty kissed his teeth, scoffing at his brother, refusing to listen to the words he'd said to him.

Now Gramps spoke. "Matty, it is a pleasure to see you, but you know you are no longer welcome at the estate."

Four's mother spoke. "I apologize, Gramps. I invited him. We had this family dinner a year ago without him, and it didn't seem fitting."

"Kimberly, I do not appreciate you going against my wishes," Gramps spoke, looking at Matty and shaking his head at him.

Now the staff was setting salads down at the table for us.

I'm not sure what Matty had taken before he got here, but his mouth was on fire. "Oh, I apologize too, Gramps." He said sarcastically.

Wiping his eyes, mimicking fake tears, he said. "I'm just such an abomination to this family. How will I ever live with myself? My grandfather hates me because I'm gay, my father kicked me out of the family business because I love to have a good time, and my own brothers won't talk to me." He forked his salad, a hearty laugh escaping him as he threw his head back and pointed his fork at Gramps. "That was a good one, old man! Admit it."

"Enough!" Their dad spoke, standing from the table. "I will not sit here while you bring shame to this family. Deal with your men, smoke until your lungs shrivel, and drink until you've exhausted your liver. But what you will not do is drag this family's name and legacy through the mud. You make me sick, Matthew!" Then, without another look at his son, he left the room.

Four's mother jumped up to her husband, trying to reason with him in Matty's defense. "He needs his family in this trying time, Matthus! We need to be here for him to become well again."

Meanwhile, Gramps had his head in his hands, starstruck about how his family dinner was suddenly going to hell.

Four tapped my forearm, and I looked up from eyeing my salad. "Let's go for a walk. My family usually regroups once the main course is brought out."

Still, it seemed as if he was not resonating with any of the events that were currently occurring. Yet I could not judge, so I allowed him to pull my chair back and left the mess behind us.

CHAPTER 14

TOSHA

His grandfather's estate was stunning. I never thought I would ever get to experience something of this magnitude while still in college. Not that I didn't wish to be able to see something like this, it simply didn't seem like I would be able to get that wish fulfilled.

Four took me down to the lake, where a path allowed us to view the garden, and what a beautiful sight it was to see. Flowers of all sorts blessed the soil with their vibrant richness and floral scent. It was soft and subtle but still electrified my senses.

We walked side by side, me being so focused on the scenery before me while Four seemed to be deep in his own thoughts. As we got closer to the lake, I smiled, seeing a trail of lights that followed the path of the wooden dock. The water was iridescent under the reflective light of the moon and the stars. Oh, the stars filled the night sky more thoroughly than I'd ever seen them.

There was something very serene about being out here. The stillness it brought me was unexplainable. It settled my nerves, and I delighted in it.

Four walked to the edge of the dock, sat down to his butt, and allowed his feet to hang over the waters. He stared out, pondering deeply. It only felt right that I took place next to him; I was his guest, after all.

"I'm guessing it's like this every year?" I questioned once I had gotten myself settled. This dress was going to war with my extra pounds, but I wouldn't let it bother me. Enough was going on as is. My dress could wait.

He nodded, looking out into the openness. "Last year, Keith and Vinny got into a massive altercation. The year before that, Matty and I wrestled with one another. We broke one of Gramps' antique porcelain vase from Germany. It's always..." He lingered.

"Eventful?" I finished for him.

Four chuckled. "More or less, yeah."

I nodded. "Your mom seems like she tries to hold everyone together as much as possible."

"She tries. Unlike my father or Gramps, she knows the importance of family and wants us to enjoy our time with one another." Sighing, he continued. "Father and Gramps are the total opposite. Their entire world is based on the family business and continuing the legacy, by any means necessary." He spoke to me, but his mind seemed far.

"What's on your mind?"

"Too much, really." He told me. "I want to thank you for joining me tonight. I know my family is a lot, and I basically blackmailed you with the phone thing on the beach, but I want to let you know that this service for me is well appreciated. You could've flaked on me."

"I definitely thought about it. The only thing that made me less reluctant to tag along was the great food and wine part. However, the only tasty thing I've had so far was a piece of bread." I said.

A smile lit up his face as a deep laugh escaped him. "The main dish will make up for the starters." I found myself engrossed with his profile, and as he spoke his words out in a deep husky tone, I felt drawn to him. "You look beautiful tonight, by the way. I like what you did with your hair. You should wear it like this more often."

I wasn't sure if I'd sat down this close to him initially, but suddenly he seemed closer. Four's chest heaved as he inhaled a sharp breath. I unknowingly mimicked his action. My throat felt dry at our closeness, and I licked my lips subconsciously. His eyes followed my action, and he swallowed deeply.

"This question may seem like it's coming from left field, but I'm still going to ask. How does your boyfriend feel about you being here with me tonight?" He said almost in a whisper.

Stunned, I answered hesitantly. "Why do you assume I am seeing someone?"

"Back there, you made a comment at Suzie regarding it. What was that about?" Four questioned boldly.

"You sound very interested in my personal life for someone who's only known me for a short while now."

"I've seemed to have found an interest in *you*."

I cleared my throat. I made it clear to Four that I would not be a conquest. "I made it clear to you that whatever you think will happen between us won't. You're not my type, and I will not fall for your charm like the other girls around campus."

Nonchalantly, Four nodded. I diverted my gaze from him to the water. My body tensed as I felt his hand brush away my curls off my shoulder.

"Hmm. You're not really my type either." The pads of his thumb traced my skin. The wind blew fearlessly, causing the aroma of his cologne to brush past my nose. I internally melted as his rich signature smell became familiar to my senses.

I needed to get a hold of myself before Four witnessed me unravel before him. Fortunately, he left my shoulder alone, yet I immediately missed his touch.

"Yeah, right. It must unnerve you to know that I can't be charmed."

He shrugged at me, looking me directly in my eyes. "It doesn't."

"Oh no?" I teased.

"Nope."

I folded my arms, causing my cleavage to jump a bit. But Four's eyes didn't leave mine. "And why is that?"

"Because," Biting down on his lip, he exhaled. "I can wait for things if they're worth it."

"You're waiting on me? To what? Let you have your way with me?" I questioned.

He scoffed, a devilish smirk playing on his lips. "I never said you were worth it."

I was speechless. We were always in a battle with one another, but this time was different. I wanted to elbow him again. How could he blatantly be such a prick? And here I was, daring to ask what was on his mind as if his brain could hold any valuable information worth sharing.

"What? Cat got your tongue?"

"Boy, screw you!" I had done a good thing for him tonight, showing up as his plus one, but now I began to regret my decision. No way was he going to drag me here in the first place to simply insult me. I'm not sure what girls he was used to, but that was not how he would ever speak to me.

I positioned myself to stand up while trying not to tear my dress but was pulled back down by his muscular arm. "What are you..?" My question was lost in an abyss.

Four grabbed me by my waist, whirling me around so my body was pressed close to his and our faces were only inches apart.

I panicked. "Four, you better not drop me in this water or so help me God--"

He chuckled while I locked one of my arms around his shoulders subconsciously. "Relax. I won't let you fall." So he told me, but it did not help with my nerves. So instead, he secured his arms around me, bringing warmth between us.

One of my hands lay on his chest, the soft material of his top moving under the gentle pads of my palm as he panted. His dark brown eyes bore into mine, and although I wanted to do nothing more than scold him for his comment earlier, at this moment, I wanted to kiss him.

I wanted to kiss this beautiful muscular man that was gracing my presence. I knew it was against everything my dad had preached to me. I knew it went against my prior opinions of him. It went against my judgments about any involvement with athletes at Southeastern in general. But as he held me in such comfort, I yearned for more of his touch.

"Four, what are you doing?" I breathed out.

"I haven't done anything yet." He said. While one of his arms held my body steady against his own, his other hand held my chin firmly. His soft lips touched my jawline, causing me to grip the neck of his shirt. Next, he arched my back into him, allowing perfect access to my skin. My body froze as he leaned down to place kisses on my exposed flesh.

"Four..." I closed my eyes. What was this man doing to me?

His fresh cologne filled me up while his strong hands protected me. I had never felt this much at peace with someone before. His body was comforting and welcoming. His touch was sincere and polite, wanting to possibly take this to another level but disciplining himself to not push anything too far.

"May I?" Four questioned in a rasp. He bit my skin, causing me to grip his bicep and his hands squeezed my butt.

The question awakened me. My eyes found Four's brown pupils, and there lay much need and desire. I found myself leaning into him, welcoming the danger I knew awaited.

The gap that was once between us disappeared once Four leaned in and captured my lips in a daring kiss. Shock overtook me, and my response was late, but soon I began to process what was going on. Finally, I shut my eyes and allowed him to lead the kiss.

Our lips moved in sync slowly with one another. Four's lips were moist and soft, and his mouth tasted of the wine we sipped on earlier. I held his head steady with my hand as our tongues played a game. I softly moaned as he bit my lip. My body was in desperate need of him. He massaged my exposed thighs as our lips meshed into one.

The kiss was passionate and gentle. We found ourselves tangled within one another for the first time under the dark night and the bright stars. He caressed my thigh, and the light hairs on my skin stood at attention under his rough hands. I moaned into him, leaning in as his tongue met mine. My hands gripped his head and massaged his soft curls.

I couldn't believe this was currently happening. That night our lips signed a contract that neither of us initially intended.

He broke our kiss after a moment of being so enamored with the desire for one another. As our sweet lips parted, he peppered childish kisses around my jawline and cheeks. Then, with a few more kisses to my flesh, his lips came to my ear, and he whispered, "I'm still not your type, huh?" He asked with a smirk. I had been too fixated with lust to realize that I'd done what I said I wasn't going to do.

With another squeeze to my thigh, he unraveled himself from me completely, sliding me off of his lap gently on the edge of the dock. Then, as if none of this affected him, he dusted his pants off and stood, leaving me feeling cold and void.

He stuck out his hand to me. Everything happened too fast, and I wasn't sure what to make of it. I took his hand worriedly and carefully stood up, making sure to not tear my dress.

He turned away when I stood to my feet, avoiding eye contact altogether. "Make your way to the valet. I'll tell my mother something you ate isn't sitting well in your stomach, so we can ditch the rest of this dinner."

Those were the last words he said before making his way back to the estate.

CHAPTER 15

TOSHA

I always had a hard time expressing my emotions. When my mother was alive, expressing my vulnerability was easy to do. I knew I could cry into her arms if I hurt myself. Her love was gentle and warm towards KC and me. She was always a peaceful person. It taught me how to care for KC whenever she wasn't around. It taught me the proper way that a parent should love you.

My mom made us feel safe and secure. But, after the accident, things started to shift. The lifestyle which I was accustomed to change. Not only for me but for KC too. Mom was in the hospital, and KC and I spent more time with our father. I learned how completely different my parents indeed were in those short months.

Dad worked long hours in the law enforcement agency, which meant long shifts and stressful days. He was losing it between his growing workload and my mom going in and out of consciousness. And having to now raise two kids alone didn't make things any better. So he would pick us up late from school almost every day. Dinner went from home-cooked meals to microwavable boxed dinners with little flavor.

Her joyful singing during our bedtime routine switched to me being given toiletries and learning how to care for KC and myself. My dad would check in our room at night to make sure both of us were still alive and breathing, then lights out. Bedtime songs stopped. After mom's accident, we never heard another hymn before bed.

The shift was drastic for me and KC. When we visited mom in the hospital, KC would beg her lifeless body to come home. But day by day, I could see my mother slowly fading away. Our dad cried a lot. He became more strict and controlling. He was paranoid, frustrated with bills, and emotionally drowning as the woman he had loved for years was slowly slipping from his reach, and he couldn't do anything to save her from what was to come.

I lost the light that my mother gave to us. Instead, I learned to take care of and protect my sister from witnessing what our father had become.

I've been suppressing my emotions for years, and now as I sit in Four's truck with my knees facing the passenger door and my head lying on the cold window, I'm trying my best to keep my walls up. I'm trying my best not to let tonight's events trouble me. I'm trying to show that I am not bothered, that what he did meant nothing and had no effect on me. But it was a lie.

I was not upset with him. I was upset at myself. I couldn't deny that I wanted him to kiss me again. I wanted him to do more than kiss me. He was attractive to me. His face, his body, those lips. I had a sudden craving for him, and it sickened me. Dad didn't raise us this way. He would be disappointed if I ever brought him home or if he ever got word that I associated with him.

I didn't want to have a hatred for people like my father did. All people weren't the same. But it was tough to not judge based on the stereotype when I had witnessed the stereotype play out time and time again.

"Wanna get a bite to eat? We didn't stick around for the main dish." Four asked me, driving at the speed of lightning on the highway.

After the situation by the water, I pulled myself together enough to make my way over to the valet. I didn't wait for him to meet me; instead, I hopped in the car and began mentally coaching myself to not let this man put his hypnotic charm upon me again. We had been driving in complete silence for about fifteen minutes now. My knees faced the door while my head rested against the chilly glass window.

I had no intention of looking his way or engaging in conversation with him. I wanted to go home, eat and sleep. If I am candid, I don't think I wanted to continue this tutoring gig with him. This wasn't the type of student-to-tutor relationship I maintained. I refused to be written off as another girl he's slept with.

Not facing him at all, I gave a sly answer. "Not hungry."

He kissed his teeth and pressed his foot firmer on the gas, causing the car's speed to accelerate. I held onto my seatbelt.

"You haven't eaten anything all night, and I can't take you home on an empty stomach." He spoke.

I rolled my eyes but kept my head resting on the window. "I said I'm not hungry," I repeated.

"I heard you, Tosh. I'm not deaf."

"Then would you stop bothering me about it?" I snapped. Not only was I frustrated with my attraction towards him, but also because he knew what he had done, and instead of acknowledging it, he made it seem as if nothing had occurred.

We were finally getting off on my exit. I was relieved to know I was getting closer to home.

"What's the matter with you?" He muttered under his breath.

I didn't answer him. Instead, I shut my eyes, trying to mentally calm myself. After the car had come to a brief stop, he continued to drive. His speed had not slowed since we were on the highway, so I knew he was going over the street speed limit. Then, as if God was confirming my suspicions, the loud sound of a police car siren began blaring behind us. I opened my eyes in a flash, stretching my neck to look into the side mirror. And there it was. A sheriff's car with its siren on.

"You gotta be kidding me." Four murmured as he finally decided to decrease his speed. He was driving slower but hadn't pulled over yet.

I looked at him as if he had lost his mind. Why hadn't he pulled over yet? "What are you doing? You need to pull over." I said.

Taking another look at his rear-view mirror, he could see that the sheriff's car was directly behind us, with its lights still gleaming and its siren still blaring. Sucking his teeth, he finally pulled the car over into the lot of a gas station.

I sat up straight, looking into my side mirror behind us. Then, turning towards Four, I asked. "Do you have any drugs in here?"

"What?"

"Drugs, Four. Do you have weed in here? I will not get arrested with a drug possession charge on your behalf." I was frantic. My father worked for the county, and I didn't want any fellow officer reporting back to him that I had been arrested with any type of drug paraphernalia in my possession.

"We're not going to get arrested." He spoke confidently.

I was stunned. How could Four be this nonchalant? "You drove over the speed limit, and we both aren't completely sober."

He waved me off, knitting his brows together as he spoke. "That doesn't mean we will get arrested. Calm down."

"Do not tell me to calm down when I'm already calm."

"Obviously not since your head is about to explode with worry from a cop pulling us over."

I snarled at him. "Well, excuse me if I am not favored enough to never have to worry about being pulled over by a cop." Unfortunately, today wasn't my day with him. He was about to see the worst in me.

Of course, he never had to worry about being pulled over by a cop. While young teens and adults on the south side were being shot, killed, and murdered in plain sight, the young teens and adults in the north were living in luxurious, safe suburban neighborhoods.

Seeing the weight my words held in the air, his eyes softened as he watched how my mood had completely hardened. "Tosh, I didn't mean it that way. I get that being pulled over by the police is alarm--"

Tap, tap, tap.

I turned away from him. He would handle this situation on his own. If they searched this vehicle and found anything, I would be the next Hellen Keller. Deaf and blind. I don't know this man. Never seen him before. Never even heard of him. I was being held against my will for all I knew.

I could hear his window sliding down. He spoke confidently and straight-forward to the officer. "Good evening, officer. Is there a problem?"

My body went as stiff as a brick once I heard the officer's voice. "Seems so, or I wouldn't have stopped you, am I right? So you know you were driving fifteen miles over the speed limit?"

"Dad?" The words escaped me without much thought. *Was that my Pops?*

I turned around quickly, in need of clarification. Unfortunately, it was a complete mistake to do so, as once I turned, my father decided to flash a glaringly bright light into the car, and our eyes met instantly. My stomach fell to my butt. Here I was, driving with a well-known football player who not only may be a bit fuzzy off drinks and speeding but was a part of the group of people my dad forbade me to mingle with.

My father's eyes held confusion at first glance at me, then looking between Four and me, seeing our attire, disapproval hovered over him like a dark cloud. I could see horns forming on his temple as his wide nose flared at Four. Then, in the most authoritative voice, he spoke to me. "Get out of the car."

I held his gaze, wishing that this was some sort of dream. When did my luck become this awful? This couldn't be happening right now.

Four was lost between us, unsure as to what was going on. Then, finally, Four spoke up to my dad, unaware he was indeed my dad. "Sir, what exactly is the problem here?"

My dad silenced him immediately. "This matter does not concern you. I'll be back for your license and registration. Natosha, get out of the car." I knew I needed to get moving fast after hearing my first name. No one ever used my first name but my mother and father. And Pops only used it if I was in serious trouble. So at this moment, I knew not to play with him.

I unbuckled my seatbelt, sighing deeply as I shut my eyes. This could not be happening. But Four's silence and the flame from my dad told me that it was indeed reality.

I stayed silent, opening the door to the truck and steadying myself to get down. I couldn't make eye contact with Four. I was too embarrassed. And I couldn't make eye contact with my dad as I was too ashamed of the disappointment that would be sprawled across his face. So instead, I walked to the sheriff's car, tugged on the passenger door, and got in.

I inhaled and exhaled a few times, knowing that once my dad got done handling Four, I would hear the lecture of my life.

"How dare you?!" My dad shouted, his voice echoing in the car. I remained facing the window again, not brave enough to meet his gaze, let alone speak back to him. "After all we went through with your mother, I've warned you about them! So how dare you get yourself dressed up for a date with one of them?"

"It wasn't a date," I mumbled. Although I wanted to correct my dad, I didn't want it to seem like I wanted to go to war with him. I knew I wouldn't win any war against my father.

"It wasn't a date?! Natosha, have you lost your forever begotten mind? What have I told you and KC all your life?" I didn't answer him, and that got him riled up. "I am speaking to you, young lady!"

"Those people cannot be trusted. They will always choose their own lives if it's a choice between their lives or ours." I spoke like an automated machine, reciting the words my dad had instilled within me for years after my mother passed.

"Exactly! They killed your mother, and the system did not hold those monsters accountable for their actions." He shrieked. "That imbecile pleaded not guilty while he was well aware of having substances in his system."

I didn't want to dig up the memories of my past. Especially not the ones about my mother's pain and suffering, which lead to her death. I knew that guy had no remorse for my mother when he crashed into her.

However, his family had money, and people from the north side with money were always above the law.

I didn't speak another word during the car ride to my apartment. Instead, I listened to my father lecture me about how my mother was probably rolling in her grave from my actions tonight. Those words hurt me. To think he would go so low to bring her into this destroyed me.

My father was so selfish when it came to her. He would only speak about her on his own terms. KC and I could never say her name around him unless he brought it up himself.

Although it hurt me, I felt guilty to be upset with him. He was my only living parent left, raising us as best as he thought he could. Of course, I was grateful to him, but it didn't make the affliction hurt any less.

My wall was going up again. The wall that protected my feelings. It was a shield against my reality.

As we pulled up to my apartment complex, I thanked the heavens that I didn't have to be next to him for a second longer. I had completely drowned out his voice and was trying my hardest to not let his disappointment in me bring me down.

As the car stopped, I quickly unbuckled the seatbelt and got ready to go. But as always, he needed to ensure I heard his final words. "Natosha, I will never see you with that boy again. Are we clear?" He wasn't asking me or trying to persuade me. He was telling me.

Clutching the handle of the door, I said nothing. Instead, I jumped out of the car and shut the door behind me. I exhaled, needing a moment to let all of my night's frustration out of my head. My phone chimed in my hand, and as I looked at it, I saw it was a text from Four.

Is everything alright?

102

I knew he probably had a load of questions as to what the hell happened tonight. Still, I didn't want to talk about it. I clicked my phone screen off and went inside, ignoring his text altogether. I knew this week we'd have a studying session, so I couldn't run away from this, but hopefully, I could convince him to put a request in with Dean Dr. Walker to get him another tutor. It seemed like the best option for us and the best escape for me.

CHAPTER 16

FOUR

"**D**ude, are you listening to me?" I whined to Trey as I shot him a look. He appeared more invested in peeling a tangerine than helping me with my situation.

The weekend flew by, but the situation with Tosha and her dad couldn't leave my mind. So I decided to extend my concerns to Trey, needing brotherly advice.

He continued to peel his tangerine nonchalantly. "You've been moping around the kitchen rambling on about a girl I don't even know."

I threw my hands in defeat. "You do know her! I told you, Tosha is one of Jasmine's friends who came to our last party."

I got his attention with that. He raised his eyebrow at me. "You're talking about one of those fine girls? Why didn't you tell me this before? I was under the impression that you and Ada were messing around."

"What? No." I made a face at him. "Ada is just a long-overdue secret fling." I turned away from him and began to pace around the kitchen again. "Would you put the tangerine down and give me actual advice?!"

"It's a mandarin!"

"They're the same thing!" I emphasized my words.

"A tangerine is a type of mandarin. Tangerines are mandarins, but not all mandarins are tangerines." The breakdown of his classifications of citrus wasn't relevant to me. He shook his head. His honey-toned locs swayed from the flow of the action. "This girl must be doing a number on you. I haven't seen you this agitated since your dad used to do those random monthly visits." He continued. "But alright, I'm listening. The tutor girl had the afro and came with Jas to the party with her other friend with the braids."

"Correct."

"And you have a crush on tutor girl--"

I cut him off. "No. I don't have a crush. I just wanted to get with Tosha to prove that I could."

Trey popped a piece of his mandarin in his mouth, smirking at me while he chewed. "You're coming to me for advice on a girl, Four; admit that you have a childish crush on her."

"Trey," I spoke cautiously.

"Alright, alright. You said Tosha's dad is a cop?"

"A sheriff."

Trey sighed deeply and popped another piece of fruit into his mouth. "My advice to you is to stay away from that one."

My eyes went still, and I stopped pacing in the middle of the kitchen. "What? Why?"

"Look, man. You're my homie, so just a word of advice. There are different types of dads you should stay away from when it comes to their daughters. The first dad is the one who follows the word of God. Their spiritual faith is strong, and they are very protective of evil forces trying to harm their children. The second dad is a law enforcement or military dad. They will try their best to dig up any information about your life and watch your every move. These dads are cut-throat and don't play about their daughters." He held up three fingers. "The third dad is street dads. You should already know this isn't a good option. Those dads lived all their lives in the hood and around poverty. They've been around the block and done many immoral things to survive. Many of them have sold drugs, killed and served time. Imagine what they'll do in the south-side if folks see your north-side behind roaming their block."

"She's from the southside."

Trey scoffed. "Yeah, stay away from that girl, my guy. A tutor girl from the southside with a sheriff as a dad? You're signing a death wish if you take her on."

"Then what the hell am I supposed to do? I can't stop talking to her. She's my tutor."

"Did her dad give you a ticket?"

I shook my head. "He gave me a warning." *A warning to stay away from his daughter if I wanted to keep my legs intact.* I took the threat seriously. I needed my legs for football.

I leaned over, resting my elbows on the counter, and roughly ran my hands through my messy bed hair. "Dammit!" I groaned loudly.

"You need a blunt. You're losing it, man." Trey reached into one of the cereal boxes and pulled out our hidden stash. He tugged at a drawer and pulled out the wrap and a herb grinder. He slid the bag to me. "Break down, and I'll roll."

I huffed but began to break down the herb. I was frustrated beyond measure. I never thought in my entire life that a girl, let alone my tutor, could get me riled up like this. Since I met her, she'd been so beautiful in my eyes, but the night of my family's dinner allowed me to see her in a different light. That night on the dock, she wasn't just beautiful to me. She was sexy. Her sex appeal exuded from her confidence and sturdiness within herself.

The kiss we shared was abrupt, and I wasn't sure why I leaned in for it. Before it, I felt Tosha had been taunting me by openly rejecting my charm. I didn't regret the kiss. I wished I had kissed her longer. Leaning in for the kiss wasn't in pursuit of sleeping with her. My attraction to her was evident; however, there was something much more alluring to Tosha than what presented itself on the surface.

Tosha was a beauty that I found to be soft, glowy, and gentle. Her glossy coarse curls framed her face well. Her skin was smooth when I touched her, and she smelled good. I got hints of coconut, peaches, and fresh vanilla whenever she was around. The aroma was electrifying.

Maybe running into her father was a warning from God telling me to walk away from the situation. Yet, despite that thought, I've set my mind on her.

She still hadn't texted me back, and I thought about sending another message but didn't want to seem as if I was pressuring her into talking to me.

I wondered what the conversation was like with her father when they left the gas station. The man appeared disgusted that I was with his daughter. However, I knew there was something more profound going on.

I needed to talk to her. I couldn't wait for tomorrow. I needed to see and speak to her today. So I stopped grinding the weed and left it on the counter.

Trey spoke. "What'chu doing?"

"I'll be back in like twenty minutes."

"Nah, man, come on. Please don't tell me you're going to see the tutor girl." He begged.

Nevertheless, I was already on the move. "Eat your mandarins in peace, Trey," I spoke to him, fleeing the kitchen and heading out.

◆◆◆

I couldn't think straight. My mind was drowning in an ocean of destructive pandemonium. Nevertheless, I continued driving until I got where I needed to be. She was my best getaway. I needed to speak to her. I needed a moment of release to forget who I was. Tosha did that for me. She didn't care about my name or my status. She gave me the best chance at not being seen as Matteo Wittstock, the son of a multimillionaire who will soon be inheriting and continuing the legacy of my forerunner.

I parked my truck in a parking space and headed to her apartment door. I raised my hand to knock, but a cloud of uncertainty dawned upon me. *What was I doing? What was my plan? Once she opens the door, what will I say?*

My actions seemed unbelievable, and I thought about aborting the mission. Yet, I was stubborn.

I huffed out, cracked my neck, and knocked. I waited for a beat, mentally cursing myself for my current irrational actions. No one came to the door after pausing for a response, so I knocked again.

"I'm coming! I'm coming!" The voice that bellowed out on the other side of the door wasn't Tosha's, but I still waited.

The door opened, and Tosha's friend, Niecy, appeared before me. I recognized her immediately, and with my eyes seeking behind to see if I could catch a glimpse of Tosha behind her, Niecy leaned against the door frame and smiled at me.

"Well, it is not an everyday thing that Southeastern's notorious football player visits you at your crib. What'chu doing here, Casanova?" She spoke, her skin glowing under the light rays of the afternoon sun.

I blinked, not knowing the proper way to answer her question. "Uh, is Tosha here? I need to speak to her." I kept it short, not wanting to tell a lie that could backfire in my face.

Niecy shook her head. "I think she went out on a date. She left a few hours ago."

"A date?" I knew something didn't feel right the night we were at the diner, and she continuously checked her phone.

She nodded. "Yeah, you can wait until she returns, or I can tell her that you stopped by." Her eyes fluttered between mine. It appeared as if she was searching for something within them. I didn't know what exactly, but I masked my disappointment well.

"It's cool. Don't worry about it. Let's keep this visit between you and me, alright?" I spoke. Niecy appeared skeptical but kept whatever she may have been thinking to herself. I was grateful for that. It was embarrassing enough that I drove here in a panic yet was given more clarity than I thought I needed.

Trey was right. I was losing it.

I needed to get a grip of myself. I said my goodbyes to Niecy, fleeing the scene as quickly as I had arrived. I whipped out my phone, knowing that although it wasn't in my best interest to do this, Ada would give me the gratification I needed, even if it was just for a few hours.

CHAPTER 17

TOSHA

Adjusting to the pain caused by parents during early childhood was something I would assume most children have learned to cope with. No matter the harm it inflicts on them or the lingering trauma that seems to stay buried within the wound even after healing has occurred. I didn't want to blame my father for what he had to endure on our behalf, but at the same time, it was inexcusable to constantly seek control over two people's lives from the guilt of not having control over the death of his beloved.

I understand the origin of the issue, and I sympathized with him. So much so that sometimes I allowed myself to create excuses on his behalf to justify his irrational behavior. Foolish of me? Yeah, I know. But he was my dad, the only parent I had left.

Nevertheless, I trained my mind to dissociate from the most dramatic events between us. It was a system that kept me from striking against my father. It was the only way I knew how to deal with him.

Sunday came around, and I texted Xan to ask if his offer to hang out was still up for grabs. I needed to get my mind out of its iced state and back into the flow of reality. I was relieved that he was available, and we met at a small coffee shop.

It was always different being in the presence of Xan. I'm not sure what it was about him, but it felt like I was a kid again with a childhood crush. It was a breath of fresh air. We talked for a while, getting to know one another, not on a romantic level but more on a friendship level. After spending some time getting acquainted with one another in the coffee shop, we decided to walk on a trail that led to a nearby park.

I tossed my finished tea in the trash as we walked side by side.

His hair was styled into two braids going down the back of his head. They were neat as if he had gotten them freshly done.

"I meant to ask you," He paused, tucking one of his hands in his pockets. "If you're not interested in doing engineering for the rest of your life, what's the purpose of going to school for it?" He questioned.

With his long legs, I had to keep up with his strides. "Um," Not many had asked me this question, as most people assumed that school was my life since I studied so hard. I shrugged. "My dad is a different character. He prides himself in my academics, so I believe if I finish school with this degree, he'd be proud, ya know?"

Xan looked down at me. His eyes were warm. "Is he strict or overbearing? Like a helicopter parent?"

I hadn't heard that term since high school. I laughed, knowing good and damn well my dad probably surpassed a helicopter parent. "A helicopter dad is a nice way to describe him."

Xan smirked. "Ahh, say no more. My dad is ex-military, and ever since he came back from overseas, it's as if he thinks we're his soldiers." Finally, someone who could understand what the hell I was going through.

"Ex-military, huh? How are you holding up?" I think Xan figured I was getting a bit out of breath with how fast his pace was, so he slowed his strides down a bit for me.

Shrugging, he pursed his lips. "When I was younger, it was pretty bad, but as my siblings and I got older, he started to ease up a bit. With so much travel and us having to get used to so many new places, I'm glad my parents found a good spot here in Ridgeport." I remember him sharing that he had two older sisters. One was finishing her last year of college, while his other sister had followed in her father's footsteps and joined the force. "Is your dad in any of the branches?"

"Oh no, he's a sheriff for the county." I clarified. This was the first time that I had openly shared the status of my dad's occupation with someone other than Niecy.

"Hmm, how's that?"

"Tough," I responded.

"I hear you. How I remembered my dad when I was younger is the opposite of how he is now after serving. Their minds change there."

I nodded. "I wholeheartedly agree with that, amongst other things."

"So, what would you have chosen if your dad wasn't so involved in your career?" Now that was a question I had never been asked before. No one ever asked or wanted to know what I originally wanted to do with my life.

Teachers at school always told me how gifted I was with mathematics and science. It wasn't only that I had to study hard to impress my dad but also that I had to learn beyond my own understanding at a young age as I had a little sister to teach at the same time. To protect her from the scrutiny of our father, I helped her with her studies daily.

Growing up on the town's south side would either make or break you. University was the best escape from the southside. But, if you couldn't get a scholarship to attend, you'd find yourself stuck there, working minimum wage jobs with high crime rates and delinquents on the streets. Not to mention the young girls who were either coked up on a dark corner or pregnant without much stability from their child's father.

"Um.." I stuttered as we came to a stop by a bench. Xan took a seat and leaned back while he stretched his arms. I followed suit behind him, not wanting to just stand there like a statue. "Since I was younger, I've always wanted to be a chef, have my own restaurant or something like that." He watched me intently as I played with my fingers, trying my best to understand what I wanted to do with my life.

"Oh, you cook?"

Turning to him, I furrowed my brows. "I can throw it down in the kitchen!" I spoke confidently, knowing that if there was something I did as good as studying, it was cooking.

He chuckled at my reaction to his words. "Alright, alright, forgive me. I didn't know I was sitting beside the next Edna Lewis."

I was taken aback. "What do you know about Edna Lewis?" I teased.

"You're not a true southerner if your grandma didn't have at least one of Edna's cooking books."

I chuckled, knowing that it was true. Not only did my granny have a few of Edna's books, but my mom also had one in particular that I would refer to whenever I wanted to learn more about the black genesis of cooking in American society.

Xan's phone buzzed unexpectedly, interrupting our time together. He checked it quickly but sighed after reading it. The look on his face expressed that something wasn't going in his favor today.

"Is everything alright?" I questioned, not too sure what had made his mood change.

He shook his head, tucking the phone back into his pocket and getting up from the bench. "I have to get going. Something happened at my apartment. I need to go handle it, but," I got up from the bench, waiting for him to finish his words. "If you're up for it, some of the guys I know are hosting at a club downtown called Storm nightclub. You should come and bring friends. The more, the merrier."

Although the club scene wasn't my style, like Niecy said, I needed to become more open to the possibility of things. I nodded to him with a smile. "I might take you up on that invite."

"Alright, I'll send you the details." He spoke, releasing me from the hug we shared. I sent a nod his way then we departed.

"Niecy!" I yelled, shutting the door and hanging my keychain on our personalized key holder. The sweet aroma of popcorn filled my senses as I came into the view of her sitting on our sofa, watching reruns of *Moesha* on Netflix.

She wore her hair in a bun. She was wearing her casual house clothes, with a blanket over her, while she held a bowl of fresh popcorn in her lap. Her eyes lit up as she saw me, the look in them letting me know she had something to spill.

"Girl, I've been waiting for you to get home." She said, tapping the space next to her.

My eyebrows furrowed in confusion, but I took my seat next to her after kicking off my shoes. I shrugged off my jacket and snuggled under the blanket with my friend.

Once I was finally comfortable, she spoke. "You need to spill the tea on what is going on in your life right now because homeboy pulled up a few hours ago looking for you."

"Xan?" *Had I missed something?* I thought to myself. "I was with him just a moment ago. When did he come here?"

Niecy tossed popcorn in her mouth, and while she chewed, she wagged her index finger to me. "No, not the computer guy. The other one, the Casanova football player."

"Four?" Now I was baffled. "Why did he come here?"

"The real question is, what happened at that dinner last night?"

I groaned in frustration, taking my glasses off and rubbing my eyes as if I needed clear vision to collect my thoughts to speak. "Girl... last night was eye-opening, to say the least."

"You gotta give it to me straight! What was it like? Did they have butlers?"

I placed my glasses back to my eyes and began telling Niecy of the events that went down last night. I tried to hold back my laughter from her facial expression, but it was too animated not to let out a few giggles.

"Tosha, this ain't funny. That family needs a lot of healing. It's strange to think of them in that light. Around town, the Wittstocks present themselves as a close-knitted family with a white picket fence." She shook her head after hearing about my experience, but she hadn't known the worst part of the night.

"I know it's not funny, but you're making those faces, and it's hard to stay serious." I contained myself. "That wasn't the worst part of the night. On our way home, we got pulled over." I decided to leave out the moment Four and I shared by the water. I wanted

115

to keep that moment between Four and me. I didn't want anything to be blown out of proportion.

She threw her hands up, almost tipping over the popcorn. "Oh, my gosh, did Four get arrested?"

"What? No, no. We got pulled over," I took a deep breath. "By my dad."

"Girl."

"Yeah, I know."

"*Girl*." She dragged the word out, her eyes wide in disbelief. "Tell me you're lying."

"I wish," I leaned back into the pillows.

"Why the hell was he over here on that side? Ain't he a southside cop?"

I shook my head. "I don't know. I was too busy praying to God in my head that he didn't shoot Four in the forehead." I sighed again. "I got a long lecture during our drive home. I haven't spoken to Four since, but he texted me. I want to avoid him at all costs."

"That's why he showed up here looking like a deer stuck in the headlights. But, then," Niecy pursed her lips and put her index fingers together. "I told him you were out on a date when he asked about you."

"You did what?" Then, holding the popcorn bowl so it wouldn't make a mess on our floors, I pushed her shoulder, causing her almost to fall over.

"What? I didn't know all this happened and that you were avoiding him." She shrugged her shoulders in innocence, regaining her position on the sofa. "But on the bright side, I would simply like to clarify that something in Four's eyes shifted when I said you were on a date. I think he may like you."

I shook my head at her. She didn't know that we shared a kiss, and although I wasn't sure how he felt about me, last night had distorted my views of him.

"No, we've already gone down this avenue with him and myself. That is not happening. I don't think taking him on as a student was the best idea. So this week, I have to speak to him and set things straight between us."

Although the thought of Four seeking me out did warm a small part within me, I still didn't know his real intention behind it. I was beginning to regret taking him on as a student. I never got this personally involved with any of my students except Jasmine. From him inviting me to his family dinner, us sharing that kiss, and now he was making unannounced visits to my apartment. I believe that some things needed to be altered in our arrangement. If not, it would have to come to an end.

CHAPTER 18

FOUR

Football always brought me back to the center of my focus. It strengthens my ability to regain physical power from my mental losses. It balanced out the confusion and chaos that seemed to mess with my head from time to time. The game kept me whole.

I practiced hard for the next three days and hit the books harder. I ran the track fiercely, mastered the field plays, and visited the gym with Trey and Bash more frequently. At night, I studied my lessons but still had a lot of trouble with specific sections.

Trey tried to help, but it was unsuccessful. Finally, Trey insisted that I call Tosha and schedule a session. However, I was stubborn and did not want to be in her presence at the moment.

After the dinner and the incident with her dad, going to her place was a big mistake. I hadn't been thinking straight. I had let my desire for her cloud my judgment on who I was. She buried my image and reputation by not caring to know me and made me feel small.

I had no desire to change my ways for someone I was not officially dating. I had been out of my element for too long. It was time I got back into the swing of things.

A knock came on my bedroom door, and although he didn't step in, Trey's voice bellowed through my door. "Aye, you up? You got a visitor, man."

I hadn't spoken back, not knowing who was here as no one had informed me that they were stopping by. So instead, I pushed Ada's arm off me, her sleeping naked body snuggled relatively close to mine. I moved under the sheets with precision until I broke free from her.

I knew I shouldn't string her along like this, but I needed to fill the void within me with someone familiar. I couldn't admit that something within me yearned for someone else because this person seemed so far out of my reach.

I grabbed a pair of shorts, slipping them on as I ran a hand over my face to rid myself of sleep. I had been winding down in the evening and took a nap after Ada came over. My body felt restless after the intense training on the field.

Still, I quietly limped out of the room and shut the door behind me. Getting down the stairs was a struggle of my day, but I pushed through it. My body ached, but the more I focused on the pain, the less I focused on the other issues that sprawled in my mind.

"Which one is your favorite?" I heard Trey speaking from the kitchen. There were a few sounds of appliances being used, but another familiar voice piqued my ears.

Tosha's voice came in like a soft melody to my ears. "I must say it's a tie between the brown sugar cinnamon and the s'mores."

"You got to try this one. It's cookies & crème."

"Is the filling chocolatey?" She spoke cautiously, and as I walked through the door frame, she was indeed there.

Her skin radiated under the light. It appeared soft, smooth, and rich. Her hair was in its usual bun with a few curls hanging free. Her glasses sat perched on her nose while her brows scrunched up at the box of cookies & crème pop-tarts. She wore an oversized T-shirt with the animated cartoon character, Taz, centered on the front. She was wearing shorts for the first time since I'd known her. They were light-washed jeans and brought out her mahogany-oiled skin.

Trey appeared fully engrossed in her and hadn't realized I stepped in, but she heard my steps and turned slowly. Her eyes were big and innocent behind her lenses. She wrinkled her nose, pushed her glasses up, and shut her lips once our eyes connected. With the sudden silence that took over, everyone was sure that something was up, and the elephant in the room was undeniable. I didn't speak, not sure what to say.

She stared back at me while I watched her. Her eyes trailed down the length of my bare chest. However, she didn't allow her gaze to drop below my waist. Instead, she cleared her throat, and I looked at Trey, signaling for him to let us talk alone. He did so, taking a pop-tart with him on the way after giving Tosha a head nod off.

Now we stood, neither of us sure where to start from the last time we'd seen each other. After the moment I'd recently experienced with Ada, I knew that anything I felt for Tosha was nothing more than lust.

"Sorry to show up unannounced," She started, shifting her weight from one leg to the other. "I thought it would be best to talk face to face."

I gave a short nod, tilting my head to the patio sliding doors. I took the lead and listened to her footsteps as her sandals tapped lightly on the ground. The fresh air from the patio was welcoming and relaxed. Fall was surely kicking in, and the breeze was picking up. I rested myself on the patio's deck railing. Tosha mimicked my action but kept a fair distance between us.

"I wanted to come here in person and speak to you since we haven't seen each other since the dinner and the run-in with my dad." She paused as she gathered her thoughts. "That night was eventful, and I want to apologize for dad's behavior. It was uncalled for." She paused again, and I stayed silent. "Four."

"Hm?" My answer was a mere mumble, barely audible.

"Are you listening? I'm speaking to you, and you don't look engaged."

"Isn't that why you came here? So that you could talk?" I spoke casually. Her time here was only taking from the time she could be spending with whoever took her out on a date on Sunday.

"No, I came here so that *we* could talk. Maybe I caught you at a bad time because your mood seems off right now."

"Maybe you shouldn't have stopped by at all," I spoke dryly, and those words seemed to provoke her.

"What's your problem? I've been here for less than ten minutes, and you've been giving me the cold shoulder!" She stepped closer, her hand flailing in the air as she spoke to me. "I came here to talk, apologize for my dad's behavior and tell you to request another tutor from the dean. Unfortunately, after the moment we shared at the dock, I don't think it is in our best interest to work with one another. I'm not trying to persuade you to request another tutor. I'm demanding that you do or else I--"

I cut her off, straightening my figure. "Or else, what, Tosh?" I pressed her.

She paused for a moment. "Oh, now you got the balls to speak?"

"I'm not requesting another tutor," I spoke sternly, turning my back to her and facing the ocean where the sun was setting beautifully.

"Listen, I don't know what has come over you, but I'm not going to keep going back and forth with you. You're immature--"

"I'm immature? Tosha, you can't be serious!" I didn't want to shout at her, but my voice bellowed more vigorously than I had anticipated.

I watched as she folded her hands over her chest, waiting for me to carry on.

"I reached out to you and went to your place to check on you, and a few days later, you appear again as if nothing happened that night with your dad! So now you're trying to remove yourself as my tutor altogether? You constantly close yourself off as if speaking to me about anything other than my studies is a crime. As if being around me for your delight is punishing you!" Her lips pouted, but she didn't speak. I continued. "Since the day we met, I've been trying to get us to know each other better, get us comfortable with one another, and you've been so strict."

"You've been trying to get us comfortable in bed." She spilled.

My response came out quicker than my brain could process it. "So?"

She knitted her brows. "Really, Four? Are we going to go through this over and over again?"

"We wouldn't have to constantly have disagreements if you would quit being uptight all the time."

"Right, you want me to not be uptight and simply run into your arms blind with myself as an offering." She spoke sarcastically, rolling her eyes at me in vexation.

I squinted my eyes. "It finally makes sense to me now how your dad is a sheriff. You're both uptight."

"Quit calling me uptight!" She was standing on her tip-toes now. She poked at my chest while she spoke, and I brushed her hand off me.

"Stop it, Tosha."

"Stop being a douchebag, Four."

"That's what I am, remember? Isn't that what you think of me based on what you've heard?" I pushed.

Her eyes wandered around my face, puzzlement fell upon her, and she lost her words.

The sound of the patio door sliding open caught our attention, and Ada stood there. She wore nothing but one of my T-shirts while her long legs glowed under the rays of the sunset. Her blonde wavy hair fell around her shoulders while she used her hand to block away the sun from her eyes.

Ah man. Ada being upstairs slipped my mind.

Tosha and Ada stared at one another. Ada glared in bewilderment as she gave Tosha a once-over, but Tosha barely stared at her long enough to start a real stare-off. Instead, Tosha turned to me, her voice low as she spoke so that only I could hear what she had to say.

"I don't think you're a douchebag based on what I've heard. I think you're a douchebag based on what I've seen." And as quickly as she had come, she walked off from me, past Ada, and through the sliding doors. Even with a half-dressed alluring woman walking toward me, something deep inside me wanted to go after the one getting away.

CHAPTER 19

TOSHA

"I don't know, guys. Something doesn't seem right with him." Jasmine spoke softly, her eyes heavy with worry as she slurped down her milkshake.

Jasmine and I had met up to have a studying session earlier. Since Niecy didn't have anything to do, she asked to join along. Jasmine didn't mind, so we all came across the street from the apartment at Benny's Pizzeria. After our study session, we all decided to hang out here and talk.

Jasmine had shared with us that Bash had been sleeping over in her apartment more often than usual, and he seemed closed off. She didn't know if something had occurred with him and the guys, but he wasn't hanging out with them like he usually did.

I was perplexed to hear this as the other day, when I'd gone over Four's place, Four and Trey seemed fine with one another. I kept that information to myself as only Niecy knew of my involvement with Four. I didn't want anyone to think that he and I were more than what we were.

Today, he and I weren't on talking terms at all. Niecy had asked me what I had done to the man for him to be so worked up, but I didn't have a response for her. I'm not sure where the root of his attitude had stemmed from, but I wouldn't entertain it. I wouldn't let my mind be consumed by the likes of him. Nor would I conform to his charms or seductive ways. He almost had me at one point. I mean, can you blame me? He's a sight to look at for sure, but his mouth was far too untamed for me to ever consider anything.

"Maybe he's having a hard time with school and football," Niecy said, dipping her cheese pizza in a mixture she had made with sriracha sauce and ranch dressing. I'm not sure what it tasted like, but the smell alone made my stomach churn.

"He told me his knee was hurting a month ago, then he spiraled." She ran a hand through her hair. "I hope he's not going through a bad cycle again."

"A bad cycle?" I asked.

"He suffers from depression. I think I'm going to talk to him today seriously about it. The last few times I asked him if anything was wrong, he simply brushed it under the wrong and said he was fine." Jasmine said.

Niecy shook her head in disapproval. "Girl, whenever anyone says that they're fine, they're the complete opposite of that. That boy is probably battling demons and doesn't want to share his pain. You know how boys are. Always in their feelings, but good at hiding it."

"Niecy is right." I agreed. "I think you should talk to him. You never know what could be going on behind closed doors."

Niecy looked at me with her lips puckered. "You should take your own advice, Mrs. Witt--"

My eyes went wide at what she was about to say, and uncontrollably, I kicked her leg under the table before she could finish her sentence.

"T!" She kicked me back harder than I did her, and it hurt like hell. We glared at each other, my burning eyes scrutinizing her. Fortunately, Jasmine was so wrapped up in her anxious thoughts that she didn't realize Niecy's comment.

I could see that something heavy seemed to remain in Jasmine's heart. So I had to ask. "Is that the only thing bothering you right now? It seems like way more is going on than you've told us." I spoke. Niecy looked at Jasmine in question also.

Although I had recently begun to give the friendship with Jasmine water to flourish, I was still pretty new at reading her. As a result, I didn't know the proper way to get her talking without coming off as if I was trying to pry into her personal life.

She ran a hand over her face and let out a tired groan. "It's this thing with Bash and another thing with my sister."

"The one we never got to meet at the party?" Niecy inquired.

Jas nodded. "Yeah, I suspect something is happening with her, but I'm not sure. We barely have spoken in the last couple of days. She's been blowing me off a lot lately, and I hear rumors of things, but I don't want to assume anything, ya know?"

"Rumors of what? Girlfriend, you better spill the tea." Niecy chimed in as she rested her elbows on the table, folded her hands together, and perched her chin in her hands.

Jasmine shyly giggled at how eager she was to know the details of what exactly Jasmine's sister had going on in her life. But Jasmine kept her sister's rumor to herself. "It's just a rumor. I don't want to give life to anything that isn't true. I'm hoping to talk to her about it soon."

As I could sense that we wouldn't know what the rumor was. I decided to switch gears in the conversation.

"Well, on a lighter note, Xan invited me to a club downtown called Storm. I think we should all go." I shared.

Jasmine was taken back by my invitation. "Xan? The guy from the computer lab?"

"He and I are getting to know each other as *friends*," I informed them. "I also want to do more this year. The start of this semester has been interesting so far, and I want the best college experience."

Niecy giggled as she took another bite of her pizza. "I say we do as much as we can this semester too. I'm down for it!" I loved Niecy because she was ready to ride through whatever as long as she wasn't doing it alone.

"Jas?" I questioned.

Jasmine pursed her lips up, contemplating. "It would get my head out of the rut from the whole Bash situation..." She lingered.

"Yes, babe. You have to ease your mind a bit. You can be there for him, but don't let his issues drain you. That's just unhealthy." Niecy advised her.

Jasmine nodded. "Okay. Should we all get ready at your guys' place since mine will have a moping man hanging around?"

Niecy and I laughed and nodded. Then, we finalized our plans with Jasmine, and for the rest of the evening, we talked about news on social media, drama with celebrities, and bonded from shows we were currently watching. I enjoyed spending time with them, and surprisingly, I was beginning to open up to them more and more as the days went on.

"Pops told you about the other night?" I asked KC as I massaged a homemade hair treatment into a back section of my hair.

KC had gotten her phone back, and while I was under the impression that she was calling to ask for advice, I was surprised by her bringing up my encounter with our dad.

"He had a fit when he got home. Said he'd almost lost you to the other side." She chuckled through the phone, her melodic laughter delighting my ears.

I rolled my eyes at the thought of my dad's words.

After rubbing the hair treatment into my scalp and down the shaft of my hair, I twisted it into a two-strand twist. I allowed the twist to rest on the towel around my neck. I was sitting in my room with a mirror in front of me and my phone on speaker.

"I promise you, KC, we weren't doing anything."

"He said bro took you on a date." She replied quickly.

I groaned. "It wasn't a date."

KC groaned. "Who cares what it was? Pops is crazy, Nat."

"KC," I tried to speak, but she cut me off.

"Come on. Be honest with yourself for a moment." She started. "He's so brainwashed and has conditioned us to be brainwashed just like him."

"You and I both know why he is the way he is," I told her.

Although KC was telling the truth, our dad was obsessed over the events that took place during and after mom's accident.

"You're always defending him. When he said all the nonsense about you and this boy, I listened like a spy, and he was delusional. I needed to call you because I was going through a similar situation, and I didn't want to speak to anyone about it because I didn't want to be judged." She confessed.

I sectioned off another piece of my hair. "A similar situation?"

She spoke after a beat. "Yes. There was a new girl at school a few weeks back. She's originally from the north side, but she moved because her parents divorced. No one welcomed her, and with dad always telling us how dangerous the north side people are, I stayed away from her like the plague. Fast forward, she transferred into my French class, and we became partners for an assignment. She asked if I wanted to eat lunch with her, but I declined."

She groaned out in frustration. "Then, I kept seeing her in the cafeteria eating lunch alone for a week. I felt bad. The next time we were in class, I invited her to lunch with my friends and me. Now she's my friend. Her mom is welcoming, and her younger siblings make me wish I had a younger sibling. Had I kept listening to Pops, she and I wouldn't be as close as we are now."

My little sister was speaking more clearly about my current situation than she'd ever had.

"I understand, but I get so many mixed signals from this guy, KC."

"How so?"

"I have a friend named Jasmine, majority of her family is from the northside, and she's...doesn't have the ego the size of a planet or flaunts her fortune around. She's humble and relatable." I smiled.

"Okay, Jasmine's cool. What's wrong with the guy?"

"He's the complete opposite of that. He plays football for the university, and his parents are wealthy. He's in the school's newspapers, gossip follows his name, and he's a known womanizer."

She grunted in displeasure. "Yikes, why did you go on a date with him?"

I added more of my mixture to the new section I'd parted. "It wasn't a date," I stated for the second time. "This guy wanted me to go to dinner with his family because they wanted him to bring a date. I tutor him, and he invited me during one of our sessions."

She paused for a moment. "The guy invited you personally?"

"Yes, we were talking on the beach one day, and he--"

"Do you like him?"

"What?"

"It sounds like you're voluntarily hanging out with him, even knowing he's this big shot football player on campus with a reputation."

Oh, she is reading me for filth. Between Niecy and now my sister bringing up the likelihood between Four and me, I wasn't sure if what I had been telling myself to combat with what I've been hearing was working anymore.

"I'm his tutor, and I keep it very professional for most of the students I've assisted. However, since our first session, he told me he wanted us to be further acquainted."

"Hmm, well, my conclusion to all of this is that the boy sounds like he wants to hang out with you, and you have been voluntarily hanging out with him, yet you're in denial of your involvement with him because you're letting dad's delusions get to you." She clicked her tongue. "You're in college now, Nat. I can't wait to graduate and go off to college so he won't be able to dictate my life anymore. I think it's time you stop letting him dictate yours."

Niecy had told me this for weeks, yet I was too obstinate to listen. I was in college. I was a new adult. I could make my own choices and create my perspectives of people, not judge them off my father's preconceptions.

"He is delusional, but I don't believe he's aware of it. He's still hurting from what happened with mom." I said.

My dad needed therapy to emotionally and mentally heal from the experiences he endured years ago. I knew something was disturbed about him, but it was far more significant than what both KC and I could see.

Still, KC was firm in her opinion of him. "Sis, he's crazy. I'm not sure how he works in law enforcement, knowing he detests all the other officers."

That was a thought I had for years after my mother's death. I wondered why he stayed in the field and played out many scenarios in my head, but the one I always came back to was this. With the outcome of my mother's accident, I believe dad wanted to make sure that no other struggling family on the town's south side had to witness what we witnessed as little girls. He tried to make a change, which was apparent, but his bias clouded his true pure intentions.

"Is he cute?" She asked me after a moment.

"KC, you ask the most irrelevant questions, sometimes."

She giggled. "Come on; you mentioned this guy is a football player. That boy must be something to die for. So what are we talkin' now? Tattooed bad boy or a rebellious yet sexy trust fund baby?"

I chuckled at her attempts to visualize what Four looked like. "I'm hanging up now. Love you, KC."

"You're no fun. But love you too."

CHAPTER 20

TOSHA

"I'm glad to see you could make it," Xan said to me sweetly as he held the backdoor open for Jasmine, Niecy, and myself.

We all finally made it to Storm nightclub. Jasmine had gotten ready at our apartment, and we drove together to the location. I kept my outfit simple, especially since I would be around a lot of sweaty bodies.

I wore distressed black jeans, a grey spaghetti strap top that came up just a little on my waist, and clear single band slide sandals. I pulled my hair back to a low ponytail and laid my edges down as flat as possible.

Niecy and Jasmine both waved at Xan, and he returned the greeting. Then, they walked ahead into the vibrations of the music while Xan and I trailed behind them.

I spoke to him loudly so I could be heard over the music. "I needed a night to wind down."

He smiled, showing his teeth, which were beautifully white under the colorful strobing lights that lit the club. "You look beautiful, by the way."

"Thank you." My cheeks hurt from all of the smiling I was doing. He was kind, handsome, and respectful. On top of that, he was smart, had a good head on his shoulders, and made it apparent that he wanted to get to know me.

"Let's get you and your friends a drink. There's a full bar. Order anything you'd like."

I motioned for Jasmine and Niecy to follow me through the drunk and potentially high bodies surrounding us.

We got a few drinks, and Xan laced his fingers with mine as he pulled me to the dance floor. "You're from the south side, so I'm sure you know how to dance." He taunted me playfully.

I giggled as I consumed the contents of my drink, not wanting to spill it with all the people I might bump into. I allowed him to pull me along with him, and as the music changed, more people began to dance. I didn't want to lose sight of my girls, so I kept them in eye range. Jasmine and Niecy were sipping their drinks and dancing with one another close by.

I allowed the rhythm of the music to carry my body away. I wanted tonight to be my night where I let go of all this week's issues and let loose for once. KC had really put things into perspective for me, and although I didn't feel as though I liked Four, that didn't mean I hated him.

There was no need to have any disdain towards someone I barely knew.

I wanted to move on from that entirely. Tutoring Four wouldn't be so bad, and it wasn't as if I had to do it until we graduated. The semester would be over in no time, and we would go our separate ways.

I allowed the music to carry me into a different realm, leaving all my worries behind me and making my body lighter. Xan held my waist, and I whined onto him, rocking my hips. The short-sleeved button-up silk top he wore felt soft against my back, and even with all the alcohol in the air and sweaty bodies around us, I could still smell his rich masculine aroma. His hands held me tight as he leaned to my ear and spoke.

"It's nice to see you out of your element." He said.

I grinned. "I feel like a weight has been lifted from my shoulders."

He turned me around so that we were face to face and held my hips again. "Have you been stressed?" He questioned.

"Um, more like I had a lot on my mind these past few days."

He nodded as Niecy entered my vision and raised her empty glass to show me she would get another drink. I submitted a finger to her to wait up. The DJ announced to the club that Xan was up next to the mix.

I looked at him in bewilderment. "You DJ?"

He smiled shyly at me. "From time to time."

"There seems to be a lot I don't know about you."

"We'll spend enough time together, and you'll learn." Then, giving my sides one last squeeze, he politely excused himself. "I'm going to start my set. I'll be right back when it's done."

I nodded, and he made his way up to the DJ booth. I found myself back at the bar with Niecy and Jasmine.

Jasmine stuck her head out first to me, her eyes wide in interest. "You and Xan, huh? Didn't I claim him in the computer lab that one day?" She said jokingly.

"Well, in my defense, you're already spoken for, Miss Jasmine."

"Touché." She chuckled.

Niecy ordered us all shots, and we all threw them back. Then, another round came, and we downed those drinks as well.

Jasmine spoke as she bit desperately into a lime. "That'll be enough since I'm the designated driver."

Niecy slipped the bartender some cash and pointed back to the dance floor. "Come on, Tosha's man is dropping good mixes."

The music switched, and more people were dancing. They were all swaying sloppily from their drunkenness, but they all seemed to enjoy their time. I followed behind Niecy and Jasmine but bumped into someone.

Thank God the person reached out just in time to steady me by the grip he had around my waist.

"Eyes up, beautiful." The voice alone was enough to make me stop dead in my tracks.

The strobing lights made it hard for me to see. It took me a moment to focus on who had their arm around me. Fortunately, I didn't need sight to know.

His deep voice, the firmness of his fingers, and the aroma of a cologne I remembered too fondly were enough to identify who it was.

"Four," I whispered his name out, and as I got a better look at him, I wasn't sure if I was ready for us to see each other again.

He wore a red cap on his head, a gold cross chain dangling around his neck over an oversized black graphic black T-shirt with jeans shorts. Designer sneakers graced his feet to tie everything together. He stared at me for a moment, his eyes trailing down the length of my body as I had done to him.

Bodies crowded us, and I didn't know where Niecy and Jasmine were. "Thank you," I said to him for being there to steady me before I tripped over myself or someone else. I didn't know what else to say, so I tried to dive back into the crowd of dancing bodies, but Four grabbed my wrist before I had the chance to flee him.

"Who are you here with?" He asked me, his eyes trying to find mine but I was searching for my friends.

"Jasmine and Niecy," I said to him, finally meeting his eyes. I pushed my glasses back on my face to keep them in place.

Someone off to the far left of us called out to him, which distracted Four. Then, finally, he turned to me, his eyes still roaming the club's environment. "Stick around for a bit. I want to see you again later tonight and talk." Then, without another word to me, he went off to whoever was trying to get his attention.

I tried to look to see who he was with, having thoughts of the girl I'd seen the day we had our disagreement, but too many people blocked my line of vision. I gave up, not wanting to appear like a lost puppy. Using my hands to shimmy through the many packed bodies, I dived deep into the crowds of people to find Jasmine and Niecy.

After a few drinks, more dancing, and frequent trips to release my bladder, the long night ended. My feet were aching and sore. Jasmine, Niecy, and I limped out of the club, following a herd of people making their way to the parking lot to get into their cars. Xan walked us out. Although he spent time in the DJ booth, he returned and joined me for a few more dances.

"You guys go ahead. I'll catch up in a minute." I told Jasmine and Niecy. They went on ahead, and Xan pulled me aside. Even as the liquor in my system had given me the courage to dance with him tonight, the nerves were still there.

"I want to see you again to possibly have another date. When will you be free?" He questioned.

"Um...I mostly tutor and have classes during the weekdays. Sunday's are usually off days for me."

His eyes were warm as I stared into them. "This Sunday is good for you?" I nodded. "Alright, seven o'clock."

"Where are we gonna go?" I asked curiously.

He smiled down at me and wrapped me up in a hug. "Let it be a surprise."

I wanted to know, but the unknown would keep me on my toes. So, finally, I agreed, giving Xan another tight hug before turning and walking to meet up with my friends who were already situated in the car.

In the far distance, I heard someone call out my name. At first, I thought I'd imagined it. But the second time, realizing that only one person calls me 'Tosh,' I turned around, my hand still on the handle of the backdoor of Jasmine's car. My eyes wandered around the parking lot, lost while people revved their engines and car headlights blinded me.

Then I spotted Four. Four stood alongside Trey and a collective of other guys. Once our eyes met, he tilted his head for me to come in his direction. I expressed the confusion on my face openly. It was getting late. What was he up to? Sensing my hesitation, he pulled out his phone and began texting. My phone then vibrated in my pocket.

His text read:

Come here.

I looked up at him. He stared at me, wondering what my next move would be. But that was a mystery to me as well. Why did he want me to go to him when we had a disagreement a few days ago and hadn't spoken?

I responded shortly.

Jas is my ride home...

He texted back immediately.

I'll take you home.

I looked up, and he tilted his head for me to come in his direction again. I took in a deep breath. I didn't want to keep Jasmine and Niecy waiting, but I was curious as to why Four was calling me over. Why did he want me to go with him? His motives were unclear to me. One day we're locking lips under the stars, and the next, he's rolling out of bed with a girl. There was a huge grey area when it came to him.

Yet something in me was drawn to him. I'm sure it must've had something to do with the alcohol, but that may also be an excuse for my desire for him. I found myself releasing the car door handle. Tapping on Niecy's window, she slid it down.

"I'm going to get a bite to eat with Xan." I lied. I didn't want to lie to Niecy, but I also didn't want to openly share that I was going with Four while Jasmine was in hearing range.

Niecy's face scrunched up, and I immediately knew she could tell I was telling a lie. But, thankfully, she kept silent about the peculiarity in my tone. Instead, she smirked, her eyebrows doing a dance as she spoke. "Alright, girl, don't do anything I wouldn't do."

Jasmine chuckled at Niecy's words. "Thanks for inviting me, Tosha! I'm glad we all got to hang out. Make sure you get home safe and drink lots of water. You have to stay hydrated."

"I will, and thanks for coming with me! Y'all be safe." I said to them, backing away from the car to allow her to drive off. I didn't miss Niecy's eye winking at me, and even as I was a bit drunk, I shook my head in disbelief at her.

I walked to Four nervously after Jasmine drove off. Not only was he with Trey, but he was also with a gang of other guys. It was intimidating. Nevertheless, a little smirk dangled on his face once he saw me coming his way. He gave Trey and a few other guys a quick dap and salute before making his way to the passenger side of his truck. He opened the door on my behalf and extended his hand to help me get in.

"Are you hungry?" He asked me.

I took his extended hand and helped myself get in his truck. I nodded to him slowly as he shut my door. He made his way to the driver's side, and I heard him tell his friends goodbye before closing his own door. It felt foreign being in his truck again. Yet, it was clean and smelled fresh like his cologne.

"What are you in the mood for?" He took off his snapback and sat it on the dashboard. He started the car, and I secured my seatbelt as he pulled out of the lot.

"A burger." It was the first thing that came to my mind. He drove with his left hand on the wheel, and his right hand was clicking on the screen of his phone to bring it to the website of a nearby burger joint. "You think you should be driving and on your phone at the--" Before I could finish my sentence, he passed his phone to me, unlocked and ready for me to begin the order. I took the phone in my hand anxiously. *What is up with him?*

"Order anything you want." He told me.

I looked at him. "What do you want?"

"I'll take a bacon avocado burger and two sides of large fries." He said, keeping his eyes focused on the road as he told me his order.

"What do you want to drink?"

"I have beers at my house." He spoke.

Was that where we were going? To his house? I thought to myself.

A bit confused, I placed the order and was glad to have put it in before the burger place closed. After placing the order, I passed Four's phone over to him.

"Four?"

"Hmm?" He was now gripping the wheel with his right hand, leaning back into his seat.

"What are we doing? What are *you* doing?" My question had an array of different interpretations. First, what was he doing with me? Why had he invited me to be with him tonight? Also, why had I mindlessly walked into his arms without much question?

He looked over at me as we stopped at a red light. "What are *you* doing?" He asked me with a slight eyebrow raise.

A titter escaped me. "I...I don't know."

He chuckled. "Sounds like we're in the same boat."

I shook my head at him. "I mean, what was your plan in telling me to come with you tonight?"

The light turned green, and he continued to drive. "I'm not sure. I don't plan much when it comes to you. I saw you tonight and wanted to see more of you. So now here we are."

"This sounds like a spur-of-the-moment adventure," I told him.

"We seem to thrive best together through spontaneity." He spoke casually.

One thing I learned about Four was that although I didn't always agree with his actions, he was always honest. I think that genuine quality about him kept me drawn to him. He told it as it was. If he wanted something, he would say it to me. There was no sugar coating it when it came to him. I appreciated that quality about him.

I decided to let all of my worries go and rid my thoughts of the last few days. Four was right about one thing. If we'd be spending ample time together, we needed to get comfortable with one another.

I needed to give Four a real chance to show himself to me. Tonight would be the start of that chance.

CHAPTER 21

TOSHA

"Why can't I have one of them?" I asked, my shoulders sulking as I pulled out my burger from the paper bag.

Four and I picked up our food and drove to his beach house. My mind raced on what was happening and what I was doing here with him. I hadn't a clue. There was something about him that, no matter what, drew me in. Being around someone who was blunt about their doings and intentions from the start somewhat bothered me, yet it allowed me to understand the situation better. That also came with the mystery of who Four was. That enigma seemed far more complex than the person I'd created him to be in my head.

We'd pass through his house briefly, and he retrieved two blankets, a pack of beer, and two water bottles. I held the bags of food and followed him closely. I had been drinking, and my motor skills were getting slightly sloppy, but I did my best to stand my ground against it. Four kicked off his shoes in the house and suggested I do the same so they wouldn't become sand buckets.

Finally, we made it to the beach, sitting under the stars while I tried to convince him to let me have one of his large fries.

He shook his head while he chucked the cap off of a beer. "I told you not to eat your fries in my car."

I frowned. Four told me this, but I didn't listen. "My fries were small. So it went like this: one fry, two fries, three fries, then boom, it was all done."

He chuckled as he passed me the first beer he opened. "Why did you order small fries?"

I took the beer and reached out my hands for the fries still. "I didn't know they would be that small of a quantity."

He pushed my hand out of his way and popped the cap off his beer. "Nope."

"But you have two large fries!" I whined.

"Yeah, because I ordered two large fries. Just as you ordered and ate your small fries." He took a swing at his beer as he unwrapped his burger.

The smell of his salty fries hit my nose, and my stomach churned. I wanted more fries. But seeing as I was not going to further beg for them, I turned away from him and tended to my burger.

Still, he taunted me. "Are you pouting?" He questioned.

I ignored him and took a bite out of my burger. I chewed my food while I listened to the melodic sounds of the waves wrestling together in the ocean. However, as I tried to take little notice of him, his presence was still infectious to me. His chuckles echoed through my ears, and soon shuffling came after. In my peripheral vision, I could see his muscular arm coming into view. I was most excited about seeing him extend one of his large fries to me.

"Here."

Yet, I kept my composure. "I don't want it anymore."

"You want the fries. Otherwise, you wouldn't have begun to pout."

I rolled my eyes at him and swallowed, clearing my mouth. "Well, if you were going to give them to me, why didn't you do that in the beginning?" I took another bite out of my burger.

"To see what your reaction would be." He spoke, passing over a few ketchup packets as he had seen me using them in the car while I was eating my small fries.

"Thank you," I said with an uncontrollable smile, taking the fries from him. "Hey, do you...do you like hanging out with me?" The alcohol was speaking.

The conversation I had with KC the other day seemed to replay in my head. Again, I was hanging out with him voluntarily, and now I questioned my own intentions. I reveled in his spontaneity and charisma, but what did he enjoy about being around me?

He grinned slowly, the creases around the corners of his eyes appearing. "Yeah, I guess." He tended back to his food. "Why'd you ask?"

"Curious about why you invite me to hang out with you sometimes," I said.

His dark brown eyes glistened under the moonlight. "What about you?"

"What about me?" I inquired back.

He threw a fry at me. "Same question; I'm curious about why you agree to hang out with me sometimes."

I dodged the fry. "My answer now will be yes, but only because you bought me food."

He chuckled. "Ahh, the food is the real reason you're here?"

I shrugged nonchalantly. "The beach is also a relaxing spot, so that's another plus too." I teased.

He shook his head at me. "I guess I'm here for decoration?"

"You think you look good enough to be considered decoration?" At this point, the alcohol was controlling my tongue.

He raised his brow, and I pursed my lips at him. "Your lips will sing a different tune in a little while." He waved me off and continued to eat.

At that moment, I got a tiny hint of gratification. The liquor brought me more courage, and I didn't mind it. Four: 1, Tosha: 2.

For a few minutes, we ate our food and enjoyed the whispers of the waves as they fanned against each other in the ocean. The quiet echoes of the wind graced us, and I felt more peaceful than I had in a while. It was pleasant.

After Four scarfed down his food and had another beer, he pulled the other blanket he brought and laid it down on an open spot on the other large blanket we were lying on. He smoothed the blanket down and got comfortable on it. His arms folded behind his head, and I watched as the muscles in his biceps bulged. While he closed his eyes to drown in the realm of the waves, I couldn't get my eyes off of him.

The man was becoming more and more appealing to me. I hadn't known exactly when it started or when I began to acknowledge it, but he was striking. His tanned skin gave off an olive undertone, while his hair appeared darker in the dimness of the midnight sky. His jawline was sharp, while his cheekbones held a natural contour. I watched his lips part, and he took in a soft air intake. His chest rose softly and descended.

Forget handsome. This man was stunning.

For a quick moment, I shook my head in an attempt to rid myself of my thoughts. Despite the effort, I found my eyes pulled to him again. My eyes went from his face down to his shoulders' sturdiness and muscular arms.

I shook my head again. *What the heck, Tosha? Get it together.* I needed to stop looking at him. I decided that instead of sitting over him, it would be best to join him and look up at the stars. I collected all of our trash into one bag and used the weight of the glass beer bottles to hold it down so it wouldn't be pushed away into the ocean by the winds.

I fixed myself a spot next to him and looked up at the stars to try and focus my mind. My eyes wandered around the night sky, but my mind was still fixed on something it had no business being set on.

"Four," I murmured out.

"Hm?" He groaned back.

For the first time, I wanted to talk to him. I needed a distraction to refocus my thoughts.

After a pause, I finally found a good enough question to ask. "Why'd you choose football over your family's company?"

"Football allows me to be myself. My family's company would turn me into Keith with a wife like Suzie, and you saw how well that's working for him." He spoke with a hint of sarcasm laced in his voice. Him bringing up that witch's name alone made my skin crawl.

"What do you think your dad thinks football is for you?"

"A hobby." He answered. His voice sounded a bit gruff and scratchy.

He sounded tired, and I was also beginning to feel woozy. However, with the partying, drinking, and eating, a good night's rest seemed perfect to end this night off.

He continued. "He doesn't see it as a sustainable career. I'm next up in line after Keith in his ideal world." I felt his body turn over, and I peered at him. His tired brown eyes connected to mine instantly. His eyes hung a bit low, and I knew he was likely intoxicated. "I allow him to think that."

"That you'll be next up?" I pondered.

"Yeah, I realized if I give him just enough, it keeps hope alive in his eyes. It also keeps me in his good graces. The hardest part is maintaining the facade of it all; the family dinners, galas, and art auctions. It's always one thing after the next that he wants us to attend to get familiarized with what our lives will entail after school." His eyes trailed my face as he spoke. "That isn't for me." What he said next would steer the conversation to a place I didn't want to go. "I am fighting the urge to touch you right now, and the way you're looking at me isn't making things any better for me."

I blinked, hoping that what he said was a figment of my imagination. Silence took over me. My lips were too stuck to speak. Unsure of what to say, I stayed silent. This man was going to start something dangerous that I knew I wouldn't want him to stop. I inhaled softly, exhaling deeply. Four couldn't hold himself back; shockingly, I was curious to see what he would do.

His strong arm stretched out to me, and his massive hands trailed against my waistline. My body responded strangely to the roughness of his hands. Instead of deflecting against his touch, I felt compelled by it. I watched him as he licked his lips and pulled at my waist, pulling me closer to his own body. From that quick movement, my hand fell on his chest. His heart was beating rapidly.

"Why...Why is your heart beating so fast?" My voice was meek.

"I'm not sure. It could be nervousness." Four answered.

"Nervous of what?" If he was nervous, I couldn't describe what I felt.

"Nervous about what my mind is telling me to do." He said.

"And that is?"

A smirk tugged at the corners of Four's lips, and I knew I shouldn't have asked by the twinkle in his eye. In response to my inquiry, his fingers roamed slowly over the exposed skin of my midriff. I wasn't sure what his next move would be. However, Four shocked me with the unexpected.

His hand dived underneath my top, snaked behind my back, and I felt my bra clamps being undone. His eyes stayed glued to mine, but I didn't think I had enough strength to look into his eyes while he touched me.

My body ached for another piece of what I'd experienced on the dock with him. The thought of him being with another woman soon after crossed my mind, but my body desperately begged for his touch. I wanted him to touch me.

"Do you want me to stop?" Four challenged.

Like a fool, all I could do was shake my head 'no.'

Four caught me by surprise, and in seconds, my head was tilted back by his own as he pressed his lips onto mine. My eyes shut as I allowed our lips to find their rhythm.

My body drew closer to his while I locked my fingers around his neck to hold him in place. I didn't want him to move out of this position.

I moaned softly into Four's lips as he bit down onto mine. My body was aroused and yearning for this man. A grunt escaped him and echoed through the whispering winds.

Suddenly, Four pulled away from me. His lips left mine, but I lusted for more. He was hovering over me with a flame in his eyes that I had never seen before. It stirred the pit of my stomach and made me want to shy away. I didn't understand. Why had he stopped?

"Four, if this is another one of your games--"

"Relax," Four spoke, reaching over his shoulder and pulling his shirt off swiftly. His body was beautiful. Each muscle was sculptured to perfection.

Should I stop this? We shouldn't have been doing this. But I wanted it. My flesh was in complete control. At this moment, I wanted Four more than ever before.

That night, Four tended to my body's needs without me correcting or coaching him. Although we didn't have sex, his need to please me in another way was very effective. He knew the right things to do and when to do them. We were in sync.

As Four devoured me, euphoria circled me, and ecstasy dominated my body. My head fell back while my intense cries were barely audible. My fingers slipped from his hair while my back arched into him. The only strength I had left was used to cry out to the man that was pleasing the life out of me.

My body was doing something I hadn't felt in a long time, and I wasn't ready for what would happen next.

"Four..." This was a warning.

My body shook in his grasp, and as quickly as I could, I pushed his head from me, ceasing all acts.

Out of breath himself, he spoke. "I'm not done." His hands were still on my body.

Despite that, I pushed him back with my foot. "But I am," Finally, I let out a deep sigh, and quickly after, my body was stable enough to submit to a much-needed release.

God, please help us.

CHAPTER 22

TOSHA

The aroma of rich seawater filled my nostrils as my eyes fluttered open. It took a while for my vision to adjust as vibrant streaks of light shone over my face. The rays of light emitted heat, not too intense, but the warmth was evident. Unfortunately, my vision was fuzzy as I didn't have my glasses on my face.

As I looked to the right, I saw long white drapes swaying by the wind blowing in from white cracked windows. I heard the gentle flushes of waves ringing in the background of my ears while the birds sang delightful tunes. My hands roamed under silk sheets, and a realization hit me immediately as I gripped the fabric.

This wasn't the color nor the texture of my own sheets. Also, I didn't have long drapes like what I had seen. I never heard the ocean's tune or smelled the salty aroma of the sea when I awoke every morning.

The room had an underlying smell of marijuana. There was no hint of smoke, but the lingering scent of weed was evident to my senses.

This was not my room. *So, where am I?*

My movements were slow. I sat up, and the sheets rested over my lap.

I scratched my scalp and felt my hair was a bit loose from the pulled-back style I'd worn last night. I had a minor headache, and my legs felt sore. I took that time to scan my body. I wasn't wearing the same clothes from last night. Instead of my spaghetti strapped top, I wore an oversized T-shirt with an anime character on the front that I didn't recognize. I didn't have anything under that. I pulled the silk sheets off my legs, and I was bare. As bare as I had been when I entered the world.

I tried to recall the events of last night, but parts of my memory were a blur. Fortunately, I remembered leaving the club with my girls and talking to Xan. He had asked me out on a date. Four snaked his way into my line of vision as we parted ways, and that is where I'd lost all of my good sense.

Shame and guilt fell over me as I looked down at my lap again. My underwear and pants were gone. I sat with only a T-shirt on that didn't belong to me. Memories of last night began to flash as I forced myself to backtrack on what happened.

The first thing that came to my head was my lusting after Four, which led to us kissing, touching, and later him performing an act on me. I didn't know how it got that far, but my drunk mind had convinced me that I wanted it. Now shame was all I felt. Shame that I allowed that to happen while I knew I was trying to get familiar with Xan, not Four's tongue.

I sighed to myself, my hands going to my hair in frustration. "Ah, what did you just do?" I spoke to myself, my voice groggy and sleep still evident.

This wasn't what I had intended when I decided to hang out with him. In all honesty, I wasn't really sure what I intended. I wasn't sure of his intentions either. I simply felt compelled to him.

I allowed my flesh to control me rather than relying on the discipline abilities I knew my mind could uphold. Four was a different specimen that I hadn't really come across before. I thought I knew Four, but I didn't know anything about him.

It made me more anxious as the rest of the night was literally a blur for me. Finally, after releasing myself, I felt exhausted and lay helplessly on the blanket. Somehow, someway, I think I may have passed out. I'm not sure at what point, but I exerted a lot of energy and felt weak.

My only concern was, did Four and I have sex? What occurred last night, to my recollection, seemed bad enough; adding penetration to the mix and not remembering it seemed worse.

I rubbed my temples gently as guilt took over me. "Why would you do something so stupid?" I muttered to myself repeatedly, trying to understand what led me to allow last night's actions.

I was so busy sulking in my own self-regret that I hadn't heard the click of the door and realized that he had walked in.

Hearing his voice made me pull my head up from my hands.

"You're up early." He said. I looked up immediately, the action not settling well with my headache. I couldn't see his features clearly since he was far away, but I could see the frame of his body.

He wore a light grey tank top with sweat spots around his chest and paired them with basketball shorts.

I squinted, hoping my voice would become more apparent than before. "I can't see you. You know where my glasses are?"

Four went to his dresser and picked up my black frames. He passed them to me. I placed them on, relieved to be able to see clearly now. I looked back up at him. His muscular arms glistened with sweat, running down his face and around his neck. A feeling I was too familiar with began to stir up within the pit of my stomach. I diverted my eyes quickly. I already made one mistake. There was no way I was going to fall into the trap again.

"Thank you," I murmured, looking anywhere but his own eyes. "Where are my clothes? I woke up to this..." I didn't really know how to approach the situation.

He began moving around the room freely. I watched from the corner of my eyes, but for the most part, I let my eyes roam around the room to see how his living space looked.

He reached the back of his shirt and pulled it over his head. I diverted my gaze as I didn't want to get any ideas.

"I put them in the washer last night and dried them this morning." I heard him say.

I kept my focus on his room and how neat it was. He had a few books on shelves organized perfectly, with trophies aligned next to frames. Plants accented the corners of his room while his walls were a clean white but were consumed with photos of his family and himself. A signed football hung in a glass frame, and a small child-like jersey was also in a sleek glass frame. A Louis Vuitton, eight-section watch case was displayed with five glistening watches on his dresser.

The case was beautiful, and the ice within it was captivating. The scenery of the serene sun rays did it justice by enhancing every diamond and every shimmer of gold.

Four was shuffling around his room, going to a door I'd assume was his closet and back and forth to his dresser, pulling out pieces and contemplating himself.

"Did we...Four?" I was reluctant to ask, but the question stirred up butterflies.

"Yeah?" He was still moving.

"Did we have sex last night?" I blurted out.

That caused him to stop. He had a towel over his shoulder and a clean neatly folded shirt in his hands. I watched as he raised his eyebrows, but he could see my seriousness after looking deep into my eyes.

"If we had sex last night, Tosha, and believe me when I say this, you'd vividly remember every detail of it."

I found myself subconsciously rolling my eyes. This is the cockiness I didn't like.

"Where is my underwear? Why am I in your bed exposed like this? Why are you sweating like you just ran a mile?" My questions all came at once.

Four stood straight as he answered me. "You passed out after we shared that *moment.*"

A little smirk graced his face as he seemed to reflect on the actions that we indulged in last night. "I carried you inside, brought you in here, and wiped you down. Afterward, I picked up our trash and got your clothes but never found your underwear. No, we didn't have sex. And yes, I left you the room. I didn't want you to wake up and get the wrong idea, as you already did." He then pulled his sweaty shirt to me at the neckline. "Every morning, I wake up early and try to exercise." His eyes reconnected firmly with mine. "Any more questions?"

"Yes," I mumbled. "What time is it now?"

Four checked his black apple watch. "Eight forty-nine." I mentally thanked the heavens that I hadn't wasted too much time sleeping. I had a date with Xan tonight, but with the events that had transpired with Four, it didn't feel like the best move to go. "My phone?" I questioned.

He waved his hand around the room. "It should be somewhere around here. I'll call it in a minute. Are you feeling alright? Need an aspirin?" Since he was offering, I nodded. He made a mental note. "What about breakfast? Feeling hungry?" Still, he was offering, and although I needed to get as far away from this man as humanly possible, it was just a meal.

So I nodded. Four's head shook in agreement with me. "You can shower here. I'll use the shower downstairs." He placed the towel from his shoulder on the bed for me. Then circled out of the room.

I sat there for a beat, not sure what had occurred. I was trying to stay away from Four, not spend more time with him. I sighed to myself. *Tosha, do not have sex with this man. I repeat, do not have sex with this man.* He already looked pretty cocky, and from remembering how exquisite our past shared experiences were, I wouldn't push anything past him when it came down to further pleasing me.

I got out of my head, grabbed the towel from the bed, and ultimately pushed the sheets off me. Then, I stepped to the door that wasn't his closet door, knowing it had to be the bathroom.

I stepped in, and the lights turned on automatically. The bathroom appeared spotless. The floors were made of porcelain marble tile, copper sink faucets on the twin sinks, and plants decorated the place. Hints of soft baby blues were everywhere, from the cabinets to little trays that held his hair and body essentials. Everything looked as if it were in the right place.

A voice came outside the bathroom door. "There are new toothbrushes under the sink, and you can use any shower gel you want." He said.

"Okay!" I spoke back. Finding everything I needed successfully, I pulled the T-shirt over my head and caught a glimpse of myself in the mirror. I was ashamed that he had to see me looking this crazy. Pieces of my hair were in disarray, and my face appeared drained.

I took a quick shower, brushed my teeth, and dried myself. I wrapped the towel around me and secured it tightly. Then, staring into the mirror over the sink, I took down my pulled-back due. I let the faucet drip a few water beads and raked them into my hair.

I did my best with my curls, and the water worked a bit to detangle and add moisture back to my curls.

Eventually, I raked my fingers through it enough to detangle and stretch out my hair. Then, I decided to separate it down the middle with my finger, twist the sides back, and combine it into a messy bun.

I exited the bathroom to find Four sitting on the edge of the bed, fully dressed, and lacing up a pair of clean pure white Nike Air Force sneakers. He had his phone stuck in between his ear and his shoulder.

I didn't want to intrude on his conversation, so I grabbed my clothes, which were now on the bed but still caught his discussion.

"No, Ma." He spoke in a lazy tone to her. "I haven't heard from Matty since the dinner either. You tried checking the apartment he used as a hideaway in New York?"

I quietly trotted back into the bathroom while he spoke to his mother.

"Next time we see him, I say we throw a tracker on his foot. It's not like he hasn't had one before."

That was the last thing I heard before shutting the door to ensure privacy. I dressed and tried not to think about what was happening in Four's conversation with his mother.

A knock came on the door. "I need deodorant, Tosh." I heard him say.

"You can come in," I spoke to him.

There was a brief pause for a second, and then the bathroom door slid open. Four was no longer on the phone, and I could see him staring at me through the mirror as he maneuvered around to get the deodorant.

Our eyes connected, and the warmth of his brown eyes revealed a tenderness within him. His curly hair was damp and not styled like he regularly wore it, but he was still undeniably attractive.

"Do you want one?" I assumed Four was referring to deodorant as well, so I nodded. As he bent down and pulled one of the drawers under the sink, one of them was filled with a tray of freshly wrapped new men's deodorants. "It's for men. I don't have any women-related products."

"Not used to this kind of sleepover, huh?" I questioned shyly, my eyes never leaving him.

He chuckled. "I'm not a fan of sleepovers." He handed me a new deodorant while his eyes burned a hole into mine. "Let's get going so we don't waste any time."

"We don't have to get breakfast if you're in a rush. You can take me home." I suggested.

He ignored me, stepped out of the bathroom, and grabbed his keys. "Come on."

"You're going to take me home?" I questioned to make sure we were on the same page.

"No, we're gonna get breakfast." I followed behind him after taking the aspirin and water bottle off the dresser.

He was out of the room and heading towards the stairs before I could get more words out.

"Did you hear me? I said you can take me home if you're in a rush."

"It's alright. We're going to get breakfast. Don't fight me on this." That was the last thing he said before he made it to his front door, holding it open and waiting for me to get with the program quickly.

CHAPTER 23

TOSHA

We arrived at a local diner and grabbed a table. I had become cold during the drive there, and Four loaned me one of his football jackets. It was oversized and hot. As we sat across from one another, I was wrapped comfortably in his warm jacket, and his scent engulfed me.

"We're always eating whenever we're together," I said after the waiter left the table after taking our order. I rose my mug to my lips and sipped my hot green tea. I took the aspirin in the car, hoping I'd be relieved quickly.

Four had ordered himself orange juice with water to the side. He leaned back into the seat of the booth. "I'm a man that likes to eat. You should know this by now." He winked at me, a smile tugging at the corners of his lips.

I almost choked on my tea. "You're gonna take this conversation down a direction I'm not sure I want it to go," I spoke.

He scrunched his eyebrows up. "Why? Scared to get flashbacks?"

"Flashbacks of something that didn't happen?" I feigned confusion. At this point, I think not accepting the events of last night would be the only way I could function moving forward.

"Last night happened." He cornered.

"I think I could sleep better at night if I stay in denial about it," I said.

He chuckled. "Denial doesn't mean it didn't happen."

"Well, I don't remember the full details to have many flashbacks about it."

Four turned around and looked across the restaurant. Few people were in our section, but the flow was picking up as new guests walked in. He then got up from his side and slid into my side of the booth.

"What are you doing?" I questioned once he moved closer to me.

"Jogging back your memory." His right hand went under the table, and I froze.

I should stop him.

However, with Four being this close and his scent filling up my space, I was at a loss of words. His muscled arm stretched over me under the table. My body reacted positively toward him, and I realized that I was opening myself up more to give him better access to me.

He turned to me, his eyes holding so much fire within them as he gazed into mine. Like last night, I felt ashamed to be so weak in the flesh whenever this man laid his hand on me.

"Take off the jacket and wrap it around your waist." He instructed with dominance.

"Someone might see us." I pleaded, hoping to convince myself somehow mentally to stop this man.

"Having an audience doesn't bother me, Tosh. They're eating anyway. No one is looking in our direction. Jacket." He said.

I moved meticulously, not trying to look too suspicious. I didn't know what was wrong with me. I didn't know why all of the senses in my brain left me whenever he touched me.

"Shh, you will attract attention towards us." He whispered against my skin.

"You're the one who decided to come on my side," I said.

"To help you remember. I'm doing you a service right now." He told me confidently.

"I'm so sorry to bother y'all," The waiter's southern accent caught my attention, and immediately my eyes opened, and I froze in shame. "I forgot to ask how you both wanted your eggs."

Four spoke cheerfully. "I like my eggs sunny side up." He turned to me. "How do you like your eggs?" His smirk told me he didn't care if the waiter knew of our actions.

I couldn't speak, let alone think about some eggs. Four turned to the waiter, aware I wasn't in the right mindset to speak. "I think she likes her eggs *scrambled*."

The waiter looked at me curiously but wrote what Four told her, informing us that our food would be out in a few minutes and something about the kitchen being backed up.

Once she left, with Four's free hand, he pulled my face close to his.

"How's your memory now?" He questioned deviously.

"My brain is too busy right now for your teasing, Four," I said, overwhelmed with my flesh and lost in a spiral of confusion. He grinned and tried to lean in to kiss me, but I turned my face away from him. "Nope, leave me alone."

"You want me to leave you alone?"

"Yes. That's what I said." I groaned under my breath while my words came out in a drowsy murmur. "We're going to eat and you're going to leave me alone before we take this further than what both of us can handle."

His chuckles rang in my ears. I was playing with fire and now knew how dangerous it was.

CHAPTER 24

FOUR

Abruptly after the game, I was one of the first to head into the showers. My body was in agony from a bad hit with another player, and my head was pounding. I knew the pain would subside, but I couldn't be around rowdy students and locals requesting pictures for their kids while I was in this much pain.

During my ride home, my thoughts fell onto Tosha. I couldn't get her out of my head from last night when I laid eyes on her in the club, on the beach, and then in the diner earlier. I didn't know my plan when I told her to come to me outside the club.

I hadn't planned to do anything last night. But, of course, that's coming from the same guy whose main fantasy has been on sleeping with her since we met. However, I knew that Tosha was different. I was not in a rush to sleep with her. But, if the moment came, it would be.

Her lips were soft, fluffy, and warm. Her body was full, and her skin was smooth. She smelled of coconuts and peaches with hints of vanilla here and there.

She was heavenly to me. To see someone so beautiful cry out into the night from my own doing was enough for me.

I didn't want to force anything on her if she wasn't in her right mind. I expected her to stop me when I first touched her. Instead, I was shocked to see her body respond the way it did, even though I knew she couldn't resist it. I caught the way she looked at me from time to time. I could see the desire for me in her eyes.

As I pulled my truck into my driveway, I didn't expect to see another car awaiting. I frowned as I recognized the car. With my head pounding as it was, I was not in the mood to entertain Ada. I had been dodging her texts and calls since last night. Of course, I knew I played a massive role in her constantly reaching out to me, but I didn't have the time or the energy for her right now. I needed to take an aspirin, roll a blunt, and fall asleep before my week officially began.

I jumped out of the car, rubbing the side of my temple. I fixed my bag on my shoulder. As I got closer to my front door, I saw her standing with her back against the wall and her phone in her hand.

Her vibrant blonde hair hung in curls down her shoulders, and she wore a natural layer of makeup with a glossy pink lip. In addition, she wore a flowy sundress that brought out her tan.

I cleared my throat, getting her attention. She looked up at me with those eager blue eyes, and her lips curled in a smile.

Ada leveled her stance, no longer leaning on the wall as she met me at the door. "Hey, I was in the neighborhood and thought I'd stop by. You haven't been answering my texts or returning my calls."

Yeah, I know. I've been avoiding you, I thought.

"I've been busy," I said, unlocking my front door and walking into the house. I kicked off my shoes while she stepped in and shut the door.

I didn't care about her being here. Instead, I was focused more on getting an aspirin, smoking, and going to bed.

I dropped my gym bag at the door and headed to the kitchen. I got the aspirin and a water bottle and made my way out.

She was still standing in the foyer, waiting for me. She spoke as I came back into her line of vision. "Congrats on the game."

"Thank you." I took a pill and washed it down with water. As I took in her appearance again, she appeared nervous, but I didn't know why. "You look nice. You had plans today?" I complimented.

She nodded, a smile playing on her lips. "Yeah, Jasmine and I went shopping. She said she's been feeling distant between us, and I think she's having issues with Sebastian, so it was only right to hang out with her for a little."

I didn't know Ada hadn't been at the game. Although I saw the dance squad, I didn't seek her out in the crowd intently. She was the furthest thing from my mind right now.

I was caught off guard as she came closer to me and rested her hands on my chest, looking up at me with her vivid ocean-blue eyes. "I know you said you'd make time for me when you weren't so busy, but I didn't want you to forget about me."

I did forget about you, I thought.

"Why'd you think that?" I feigned confusion.

She shrugged. "It worries me when we don't keep in touch." She reached and squeezed my bicep, and I gently winced at the pain that shot through me. Then, seeing my reaction to her touch, she panicked. "Oh my God, I'm so sorry. Are you in pain?"

"It'll go away in a few days," I said casually. It was the gift of the game. I was used to it. "I'm gonna go upstairs and lay down for a bit."

"I could give you a massage if you're up for it." Her big eyes peered up at me, desperately needing to be with me.

"Alright, I expect you to have magic hands, Ada. I'm counting on good results." I said as I led the way to my bedroom, and she followed, her soft giggles echoing throughout the hall.

"How's that feeling?" She asked me as her knuckles deeply rubbed my temples. We'd shared a blunt, and it mellowed my aggravation and eased my mind off of the pain. Ada worked on my back at first, then my arms, and now she was doing different techniques to help relieve any aches I felt in my head.

I hadn't known where she learned this stuff from, but I didn't ask. All that mattered was that she was making me feel better.

"Really good," I replied, my eyes shut while I listened to the distant sounds of the ocean.

She continued to rub my temples using more techniques, and now, I was thankful that she had shown up. This was soothing me, and the more she rubbed, the more I was beginning to drift into sleep.

We did that for a few more minutes until she switched positions. She gently took my head off her lap and placed it on the bed. I was so tired I wasn't focusing much on her motions, but I was still vigilant with the sounds. Finally, I could feel her moving around the bed, and once I felt her hands go to the strings of my shorts, my body froze, and my eyes opened.

She was hovering over me with her hands, undoing the string of my shorts.

"Ada..." *I was not expecting this.*

"Shhh, shut your eyes and try to relax." She spoke gently.

Lust overwhelmed me as she began pleasing me but I couldn't thoroughly enjoy any of it with the image of her in my head. Instead, I imagined that someone else was pleasing me. I desired to have someone else in her position with their hands around my body.

Tosha.

It was sick of me to think of someone else while Ada willingly pleased me, but it was a thought that I couldn't shake. So I imagined it.

With my eyes tightly shut, I imagined that Ada was Tosha and ignored her pleas to glorify myself. My ego was in complete control and I willingly allowed myself to be driven by my flesh.

I'm not sure how long I made love to the fantasy of Tosha, but once finished, my eyes opened tirelessly, and only then could I see that the woman in front of me was not the woman I was making love to in my head.

Although sex was in my biological nature and design, the guilt and shame of my actions made me feel sick within.

I sighed deeply and thought, *I need Tosha.*

CHAPTER 25

TOSHA

Later on Sunday afternoon, I texted Xan and told him I wasn't feeling well from last night at the club. It felt horrible lying to him; however, I couldn't face him tonight for our date after what I had done with Four on Saturday night and Sunday morning. When the server returned with our food, I could barely eat. Yet, Four scarfed his meal down with ease.

Guilt was eating me alive. Of course, I was single, and I would assume Four was too, even with me seeing that blonde at his place that one day. He was not known to have girlfriends or date anyone. Despite that, I felt wrong for my actions, knowing I wanted to pursue a relationship with Xan.

My guilt increased when Xan offered to bring over a cup of tea or soup if I felt too sick to consume anything too heavy for my stomach. I mentally slapped myself. I'm not sure what was going on with Four and I, but whatever it was, it ended today.

I declined Xan's offer of tea or soup as I couldn't witness his face. I needed time to get Four out of my system. He seemed like a bad addiction. No matter how many times I tried to walk away from it, my desire for it only grew. I couldn't have the thought of my lust for Four lingering in my head.

After Four dropped me off home, I snuck in as quietly as possible. Thanks to my luck, Niecy wasn't out of her room, and I didn't have any questioning eyes awaiting me. I made it to my room in peace and took another shower. I not only needed to get his smell off of me, but I also needed to get the evidence of our wrongdoings off of me.

I washed my hair while I was at it, listened to music, and busied myself to not have my thoughts trailing after the idea of Four.

Following my extensive hair routine, I sectioned my mane into four significant parts and twisted my curls. I left them that way to dry, and then I started studying for my classes. I kept my head in the books for what seemed like hours. Hunger didn't creep up on me, surprisingly, since I hadn't eaten much for breakfast, but I was able to manage throughout lunch and closer to dinner.

Niecy knocked on my door and stuck her head to tell me she was starving.

"I like how you snuck in here thinking you were slick." She started with a friendly smile on her face.

I waved my hands to her. "I did not sneak in."

"Yeah, yeah. Lie to someone else, not me, alright? But I'm hungry, and you said you'd make your bomb baked mac n' cheese this week." She pouted her lips and did the puppy dog's eyes. "Can you make it tonight, please? I'll cut up some vegetables for our sides and be your sous-chef for the night."

I couldn't say no to her when she did the puppy dog eyes. It always reminded me of when KC wanted something when we were younger. It poked at my soft spot. I agreed and placed my books aside on my bed.

She jumped up in eagerness as she saw me get up from my bed.

Niecy enjoyed my cooking, and I didn't mind cooking meals together. I enjoyed creating new recipes or perfecting meals I've made before. As cooking was something I fancied, I was glad to have Niecy with me to try out my food and give constructive criticism. She told me numerous times that if I ever wanted to give up school and become a chef, she'd invest whatever money she could in helping me with my new career.

Although we joked about that from time to time, in the back of my mind, it did seem like something I'd be interested in. Of course, I knew my dad would disapprove of it, so I would finish school to obtain my degree, but I wanted to keep at least a bit of hope for later on in life. Then, I could retire and create my own small restaurant in loving memory of my mother.

"Okay, so we got half a bag of mozzarella cheese, but there's a new bag of cheddar here." Niecy began pulling out the ingredients we needed while I pulled out the pots and bowls I needed to cook with.

She looked at me as she pulled things out of the refrigerator and set them down on the counter. "Did you enjoy your night with Four?"

Her words caught me off guard. "I wasn't with Four last night. I just—"

She cut me off. "You think I didn't see you in the side view mirror of Jasmine's car skipping to Four and his posse?" She questioned.

My eyes widened. "Oh my God. Do you think Jasmine saw me?" I blurted out.

She shook her head as she shut the refrigerator after pulling out everything we needed. She took the pot from my hands, ran it under the sink, and let the water run. "No, she was too busy calling Bash to notice. So what happened last night?"

I shrugged nonchalantly. "We got food and talked."

Despite my effort to keep it simple, Niecy wasn't buying it. She raised a perfectly arched eyebrow to me. "You spent the night over there, T. Four is one of Southeastern's star athletes, and you're telling me he didn't try to make a move on you?"

I turned away from her questioning gaze, grabbed the pot of water she had filled, and set it on the stove, turning up the temperature to let the water boil.

However, my silence only gave her more insight. "You guys did something, didn't you?"

I stayed silent as I washed my hands. I didn't want to lie to Niecy as she was my closest friend, hell, I would even say she was my best friend, but I also didn't want to talk about the events of this weekend.

Talking more about it would make everything feel real, especially with Niecy. Talking about it would solidify the actions he and I took. It would make it concrete and evident that something was happening between us. I denied it in my head. I denied it in my heart. But deep within, I knew the truth. I had an unfortunate desire and longing for a man I shouldn't be with.

I needed to keep myself busy. I couldn't think about this right now. As I used studying to distract me, cooking would do the same. So I grabbed a couple of mixed vegetables to give them a good wash before using them.

I sighed and prepared myself to speak after a moment of silence between us. "We shared a moment, and now I'm more confused than ever." I left the veggies alone and sat on one of our bar stools.

She sat on a stool and faced me, wanting me to know I had all her attention. "Why are you confused?" She inquired.

I attempted to pat my hands dry on my shorts to get my blood flow going to properly execute this dialogue to her. "It's like my world was turned upside down when Four walked into my life. I was and still am interested in Xan, but I also feel an attraction towards Four that I don't want to be there." My lips drooped into a pout.

She immediately waved the thought of Xan out of the conversation once I brought him up. "Who cares about Xan? You've had a crush on Xan since your first year, and he hadn't made a move on you. So now that you and Four have a thing going on, he magically begins to take an interest in you? He sounds very questionable. Either he had a girlfriend before, he's not into women, or he's simply not into you."

"You really think he's not into women?" I questioned.

"I don't know. No doubt, Xan is cute, but something is off to me." She clapped her hands. "Whatever it is, it isn't my concern. I am in support of team Four."

I furrowed my brows at her. "There is no team Four."

"There is now. I just created it." She protested.

"I still like Xan. I think he's a nice guy." I counteracted.

"But Xan isn't Four, T." She said with a smirk.

I shrugged. "You're right. Xan is nothing like Four. Maybe that is why I like him."

She sighed in agony, and even as I understood the powers Four possessed, it was all sexually. There was no real intimacy between Four and I other than sex. I craved a deeper connection. Xan and I were developing that connection.

Niecy disagreed with me pursuing the path with Xan, but that was a risk I had to take. If I listened to what my flesh wanted and gave in to Four's advances, I'd just be another girl on his hit list.

CHAPTER 26

TOSHA

After my talk with Niecy, I decided to reach out to Xan during the week to reschedule our date. Xan told me to meet him at The Strip, a shopping center close to campus. Ridgeport Mall was there surrounded by restaurants. It wasn't my routine to visit as most stores and restaurants in that area were expensive. I didn't have extra money to spend on things of that sort, and whatever money I did have, I used it towards groceries or miscellaneous everyday items.

I wore an elegant off-the-shoulder cream top with dark blue jeans and tan strappy sandals. I wasn't sure how to dress up for a formal date as I hadn't had a serious boyfriend since high school.

I wore my hair in a twist out and fluffed my curls. I stuffed a pair of studs in my ears, coated my lips with gloss, and used mascara to bring out my lashes.

I took the bus to The Strip as Xan told me he had car troubles the following day. Once I got there, I waited for Xan at the front of the restaurant he picked for us. I leaned against a pole, watching as people entered the restaurant. My phone vibrated in my hands. I hoped it was Xan updating me on his whereabouts. But to my surprise, it wasn't Xan.

It was a text from Four.

The text read: *Up for a tutoring session tonight?*

I looked down at the text for a moment.

He wasn't asking me to hang out with him or see him for personal gain. This was him requesting help for his studies. I texted him back accordingly.

I am busy right now. So I'm not sure when I will be available.

He responded back shortly.

I can wait.

It was still early in the evening, and although I didn't want to see Four, I couldn't deny him a study session.

"Sorry to keep you waiting." I heard Xan's voice creep up behind me. I turned around and locked the screen of my phone.

"No worries. I haven't been waiting long." I assured him, and my lips formed a smile as he reached out to give me a hug.

He stretched out his hand for me. "Let's head on in before we lose our reservation

We walked hand in hand, checked in, and the host walked us to our table.

The gentle sound of serene jazz filled my ears as Xan pulled my seat out for me. I thanked him nervously, stuffed my small clutch in my lap, and picked up my napkin to lay it on my lap.

The restaurant was cozy yet elegant.

"You look beautiful. I forgot to tell you that when I first saw you." He said as he got comfortable in his own seat.

I smiled up at him. "Thank you, and you look very handsome." I complimented back. "What are you planning to drink?" I asked him.

"Water will do." He said.

I nodded to him. "There's not much on the menu. Is this all they have?"

He shook his head. "I heard the owners are doing a menu revamp, so this is the only selection for a few weeks."

I frowned. I didn't mind the trim meal options but wished there were more appetizers to choose from.

The waiter came soon after, and we ordered our drinks and placed an order of chicken wonton tacos. Xan wanted onion rings, but I immediately talked him out of that. That wasn't a good choice for a first date. Funky onion breath on either of us would be unpleasant.

"I'm glad you came to the club the other night." He said, sipping his water.

"Thank you for the invite. I'm really shocked that you DJ'ed." I told him.

He grinned at me. "I'm into computers for the most part, but I also love music. I began producing music in high school after my dad purchased a new computer software for my 16th birthday."

The waiter snaked her way back to us and dropped down our appetizer. It smelled delicious. While she was here, we gave her our food orders. I took a taco and set it on my plate.

"Producing got me into the DJ world." He also took a taco and put it on his plate.

"Do you work in a studio as most artists do?"

He smiled. "You could say that. I created my own studio in my apartment. Of course, I don't have all the equipment, but a man's gotta start somewhere, you know?"

The evening went smoothly, with us sharing our experiences with one another. Xan was his stage name for music. He didn't think his full name, Alexander, would be catchy enough once he got big. However, he's been using that nickname since high school, and it stuck with him as he developed his music career. He played a few beats for me, they weren't my cup of tea, but they weren't awful. I enjoyed softer, mellow songs, while his tracks had a more hip-hop or pop style.

We got our food and ate while we talked. I learned that Xan liked comic books and deconstructing encrypted codes in his free time. It was a breath of fresh air to be around someone simple in all ways yet still engaging. I hadn't noticed the time flying by until my phone vibrated in my lap. Four was calling me. By this time, Xan and I had finished our meals and were waiting for the check. I excused myself from the table and told Xan I would freshen up in the ladies' room. My phone was still vibrating in my hand, but I didn't answer until I was safely in one of the stalls.

"Hello?"

He sounded dazed as if he had just woken out of sleep. "Are you still busy?" I checked the time on my phone. It was now approaching nine o'clock.

"I'm almost done," I said back.

There was shuffling on his end of the phone. I assumed he was adjusting it to his ear. "What's that sound? Why are you listening to elevator music?" He questioned.

Could he hear it? My eyes wandered around as someone walked into the restroom.

"It's music from the place I'm in. I'm not home right now."

He paused for a moment, then asked, "Where are you?"

"At a restaurant."

"By yourself?" He inquired. Why was he so interested in the details?

"No, I'm with a friend." I kept it vague. It was none of his business on who I was here with.

"Send me the address." He said.

"I'm not done yet—"

174

He cut my words off. "That's fine. Send me the address." And with that, the line disconnected, and his voice was gone from my phone.

I unlocked the stall and washed my hands. Even though I hadn't used the restroom, I wanted it to appear to Xan that I did. So I air-dried my hands and made my way back out. I saw the waiter set down two checkbooks at the table, and Xan thanked her.

As I made my way to the table, he held up one of the checkbooks. "This is your bill."

I furrowed my brows in confusion. "My bill?" I questioned. I was sure that Xan had asked me out on this date and specifically chose this restaurant for us. But unfortunately, I had been under the impression that if he set up the date for us, he would pay for our tab combined.

"Yeah, your meal was more expensive than mine. I told the waitress to split it, of course." I stared at him dumbfounded as he slid cash into his checkbook and left it on the table. Then, finally, he stood from his chair and gazed at me. "Should I walk you out?"

I wasn't sure what to say. I was beyond speechless. We'd shared a great dinner with good conversation, and things weren't ending as I expected. A frown graced my face as I held up the checkbook to Xan.

"I'm sorry. I don't mind paying for my own tab, but I was under the impression that this would be a date, no?" I had to ask the question that pierced my mind. If his intention wasn't to take me out on a proper date, why did he ever fix his mouth to ask me? Having to pay for my own meal wasn't the issue. The principle behind his actions was what bothered me most.

He feigned confusion. "You didn't ask me what you could order."

"This was to be a date, Xan. I didn't expect to have to ask you what I am allowed to eat."

The waitress returned to our table and looked between us as she picked up Xan's checkbook. "Are you both ready to close out?" She questioned sweetly, but as I was annoyed and disappointed in Xan's actions, I couldn't return her kindness. So instead, I fished through my clutch and pulled out enough cash to cover my bill and tip the waitress.

"Any change?" She questioned. I shook my head no.

"Should I walk you out?" I heard him ask again.

I barely gave an audible answer. "I'll be fine."

He tried to hug me, but I instantly pulled away, repelled by his actions. Sensing my discomfort, I could see something flash within his eyes. "Do you have a ride to get home? I want to make sure--"

"I'll be fine," I answered again.

He hesitated at first but didn't push it as he could see that I was totally disengaged. "Okay, text me when you're home, and don't be a stranger." He said, and he went about his way with a squeeze to my elbow.

I watched as he walked away, disbelief weighing me down heavily. I then pulled out my phone and texted Four the address to the restaurant. I exited the restaurant, and once Xan was entirely out of my view, I could breathe again. I relaxed and leaned on the pole, contemplating what had happened moments ago. I couldn't believe he'd pull something like that.

Niecy had been right. Something was off about Xan that I hadn't seen before. As I waited for Four to arrive, the events of what occurred replayed in my head.

A few minutes passed, and I saw his truck coming my way. The vehicle appeared more polished than I remembered it. He stopped in front of me, and as I saw his door opening, the nerves took over me.

He came out with a cap that shielded his eyes, wearing a white T-shirt that clung to his body like a glove while gym shorts rested on his waist. He wore socks and slippers on his feet. He appeared comfortable.

He walked around the other side of the car and held the passenger side open for me. I followed him and climbed in. Then, shutting my door, he jogged back to the other side and climbed in. He turned the air conditioner on and leaned back into his seat while his right hand tightened against the wheel.

Finally, he spoke as he pulled out of the plaza. "You enjoyed yourself?"

"Hm?" I questioned.

"With your *friend*?" He dramatized the word "friend."

I turned away from him and peered out the window, looking at all the cars we were passing by. "Yeah." My answer was short and curt.

I was beyond annoyed with how my night ended with Xan. It wasn't Four's business to worry about, and I was embarrassed to share it. "Can we swing by my place, please? I need to switch out of these clothes and get a few things."

He nodded to my request and turned the radio on. For the rest of the car ride, I was stuck in a bubble of raging thoughts.

CHAPTER 27

TOSHA

"How is that wrong, Tosha? I've been working on this problem for almost fifteen minutes!" Four bellowed out in frustration. He crumbled the scrap sheet of paper that he had been working on previously and shoved his laptop off of his lap.

After the disappointing dinner with Xan, Four swung by my place, where I then switched clothes and got my bag for school work. Since the stunt Xan pulled at the restaurant, my mood had shifted immensely. I was surprised to know that Four's mood had also changed. However, when I focused heavily on my work to distract me, his classwork only caused him to become irritable.

We sat in his living room. He positioned himself on the couch while I set myself up on his comfy recliner chair. I had been reading through my textbook and periodically checking on him to make sure he had understood the techniques I explained prior. As he told me that I tend to work at a quick speed, I refrained from pestering him. This lesson was a bit tougher than the last and mainly dealt with graphing. I realized that graphing was an aspect of the course that he struggled with.

I set the textbook down on my lap and stared at him. He had taken off his baseball cap after getting the first few answers incorrect, and now he was rubbing his hands in his curls viciously.

"Four," I called out.

"What now?" He snapped.

My eyebrow raised as his fiery brown eyes met mine. Soon, his eyes softened, and he rubbed one of his big hands over his face. Then, leaning back into the couch, he turned his head upwards with shut lids.

"My calculations aren't adding up correctly. I got the same answer twice, but the graph was wrong. So either there is something wrong with the problem itself, or the graph is screwed." I could visibly see that he was trying to calm himself.

Getting up from the recliner, I made my way over to him. I grabbed his laptop, sat it on my lap, and grabbed a fresh sheet of paper.

I handed him a pencil. "We'll start over from the beginning, alright?" I tapped at his knee to bring him back to Earth.

With me not leaving his side, he took the pencil from my hand, and I began to reteach the section of the lesson he was having trouble with. I explained to him the error in how he was plotting the graphs before. We sat together and worked from scratch on the problems he kept getting wrong until he got the correct answer and graphed everything properly.

"This is the last one," I said once we had thoroughly reassessed his assignment.

Although this was the last problem in his assignment, he stood up from the couch and stretched his arms instead of getting it out of the way and completing it.

"What are you doing? Sit down so we can finish." I said, dumbfounded on why he thought this moment was the best time to get up when we were only one problem away from calling it a night.

Be that as it may, Four always did as he wanted. He began walking out of the living room, throwing his words behind him. "I need a drink."

I didn't know what he meant by "a drink," but I followed him. I paused by the kitchen counter, leaning on it for support. He went to the refrigerator and pulled out a bottle of water, turning around, he caught me staring at him.

"You want one?"

I shook my head. "No, thank you. I would appreciate it if we could go back and finish for the night."

"Why? Do you have somewhere you need to be?"

I furrowed my brows at him. I didn't know the time, but I assumed it had to be well past 11pm since it was getting dark. "Where would I go at this hour on a weekday?"

He shrugged as he opened his water bottle and began to guzzle it down. "I'm not sure. You seem like you are in a rush to call it a night."

I wasn't trying to rush him, but I didn't want to stretch our time together further than what it needed to be. I knew that Four was unpredictable, and I didn't want to fall into anything that was sinful that I would regret again.

I brushed his words off and folded my hands over my chest to hold myself.

"I'm not in a rush, Four. I think it's best if we don't take breaks and stay in game mode while the information is still fresh." At that moment, a thought came to my head. "Speaking of game mode, do you have trouble reading your plays for the field when you are in practice?"

He set the water bottle down and peered down at me. "What do you mean?"

"You know when your coach goes over where you need to be and how the game will go. Doesn't he use numbers for the plays?" I inquired.

Four shook his head. "Not all of the time. He mostly uses letters and keeps it simpler to read for most of the players."

If Four was having a hard time with numbers, I would assume his game would be off if his coach did his play-by-play with numbers.

Four continued speaking. "I think a lot of the guys prefer it over numbers. Too many head injuries have most of us brain dead." He joked.

Although I didn't think that was funny. I actually thought it was pretty dangerous. "You think you're becoming brain dead?"

He shrugged nonchalantly. "Possibly. I wasn't always terrible at math. I struggled a bit in high school, but I think football has made it worse."

"Why keep playing if it's hindering your learning capabilities?"

He began to approach me, his water bottle tightly in his grip. "When I signed up, I knew the risks and damages it could cause."

That wasn't a good enough answer for me. "You're okay with possibly going brain dead for it? What's so good about the game that has you ready to risk that?"

He got closer, standing directly in front of me, and placed his water bottle on the counter next to me. "Football is the only consistent thing in my life. Unfortunately, my family is unsteady, girls come and go, and many people can't be trusted as they seem to like the version that circulates around town and campus."

I stared into his brown eyes through my glasses, and as he began to inch closer, I nervously pushed my glasses back on the bridge of my nose.

He placed both hands on either side of me on the counter. My breath hitched, but I kept my composure. "Maybe you should find something else to be consistent in your life, so you're not reliant on the game too much."

He leaned down into me, his broad shoulders blocking out anything from my vision line behind him. I took my hands down from where they rested over my chest. I leaned back, my backside hitting the edge of the counter.

"I think I've found something else to be consistent in my life." His voice was raspy as one of his hands came out and caressed the side of my face. "Rather, someone else."

As if it were natural to me, I leaned into his touch as he rubbed the pads of his thumb against my cheeks in the most delicate way.

"Hmm," I hummed out. "And who exactly is it?" I asked, aware that he was beginning to cloud my thoughts, and I didn't really know what could possibly happen next.

Grabbing my head into his hand, he spoke softly. "You." In a quick motion, he pulled my chin up to him and smashed his lips into mine.

In my right mind, my initial reaction would be to push him off and scold him for pushing himself onto me like this. However, I wasn't in my right mind, and Four didn't give me the adequate space and time to properly access and analyze what was happening here. So I went in for it, leaving my most rational thoughts behind me and walked into another cycle of sin.

CHAPTER 28

TOSHA

Our lips moved in sync with one another, and his lips felt chilled from the water he had been drinking. As our lips tangled together, I stood on my tip-toe for better balance. I believed he sensed this as I felt his hands around my waist, trailing down my sides until they rested upon my backside. I moaned into his mouth as our lips intertwined, and soon I felt him lifting me up and setting me down on the counter.

My mind was going crazy. What was I doing? I had left a date with Xan, and now I am lip-locking with Four. But I didn't want to stop.

My body felt compelled to him. I loved how his hands gripped and massaged my backside while his tongue played a game with mine. I found myself wrapping my legs around his waist, pulling him closer to me as my hands held onto his biceps to keep him in position.

That action seemed like a mistake, a for sure sin, but my body yearned for more.

As he rubbed against me, my body began to melt with longing. "Four," I moaned out. Four broke our kiss, and his lips trailed down my jawline and neck, delivering sweet kisses onto my skin.

He bit down on my lip and hoisted me off the counter. I yelped and secured my legs around his waist while my arms wrapped around his neck. He carried me out of the kitchen, but I didn't open my eyes to see where we were going. Instead, I continued kissing him, clinging to him as he carried me.

I knew engaging in this with him was wrong, but my flesh wasn't strong enough to put an end to it. He'd pleased me so well on the beach and in the diner. Knowing that he genuinely pleased me sexually seemed to make me gravitate toward him. It drew me in. He took control, and his dominance was sexy. He didn't have to tell me who was in charge. He showed me.

He tightened his grip around me as we stumbled on the stairs. The need both of us carried for one another was obvious.

Four possessed something about him that allured me to him. He had a certain quality: I always seemed to run to him instead of away. I mentally scolded myself for not having the self-control I thought I had. But, on the other hand, he knew the right things to do to keep me wanting more.

He carried me into his room and laid me down on the silk sheets that covered his bed. Deep inside me, I knew our situation might not last for too long, but at this moment, it was just him and I.

We continued on that evening, taking turns to please one another in private. No one knew what this night would make for either of us, but our lack of discipline or self control willed our flesh to take over. Moments had gone by and it seemed as if it was just Four and I. That is, until a voice was heard in this midst of our relations.

"Ayo, Four!" I heard a voice call out inside the house. I immediately stopped my actions but Four didn't pause with his task.

I was trying to focus, but the sensations of self indulgence overwhelmed me.

Four was going to ruin me, and I knew I should stop him, but I couldn't. I wanted him desperately. I thought I heard something, but maybe it was my imagination. So I carried on until I heard more noise coming from inside the house. I stopped again.

"Four!" I whispered-yelled.

He was busy. "Hm?"

"I think someone's here," I spoke up.

Four immediately paused from his actions. We both got quiet, suspiciously listening to hear closely. The silence was the only thing that greeted us back.

"No one is here, Tosha." He tried to assure me.

"I heard something," I said. I knew I wasn't crazy. Yes, I have made a lot of rash actions over these last few weeks, and that made me a little crazy, but I did hear something.

Despite my efforts, he didn't believe me. "Relax, no one is here." He said again to me.

Maybe I am a little paranoid. Relax, girl. Just as Four said, no one is here. I mentally calmed myself down and allowed my body to move at Four's tempo.

As we finally met our peak, the voice came back, but it was closer this time. So close that I didn't have a chance to stop.

Trey barged into the room with a bag in his hand as he spoke, completely oblivious to what we were currently doing. "Man, what the heck are you doing in here? I've been calling your phone—" Then Trey finally looked up and saw us.

Everyone froze.

Trey's eyes went to the sight before him and Four and I, wrapped up in one another, couldn't get our eyes off Trey.

In an instant, Four threw a pillow at him, separating our forms entirely.

Trey immediately turned out of the room, dodging the pillow. "Ah, man! My bad, y'all! My bad!" Trey shuffled to shut the door, and once he did, Four's swear words filled my ears.

I pulled back, embarrassment washing over me like a dark stormy cloud. Another man just walked in on Four and myself, and although we hadn't entirely indulged in penetrated sex, we were still intimate with one another. What made it worse was that we were both as naked as the day we were born.

Shame wasn't the best word to describe what I was feeling. I was disgusted with myself, as I thought Trey would assume I was merely another one of the girls that fell for Four's tactics and charm.

I pulled away from Four, searching for my clothes. I needed to leave now.

Four saw me shuffling in such a panic that made him ask me, "Tosha, wait, wait. What are you doing?"

"I want to go home." I quietly replied.

Four immediately tried to soothe me. "Hey, hey, hey. Trey's not gonna think anything of it. This isn't the first time this has happened."

Did he really think that was what I wanted to hear right now?

"And that's supposed to make me feel better?" My tone changed significantly, and I wanted nothing more than to get away from all of this.

He palmed his face, realizing what he'd spoken. "That came out wrong. Come here. Trey won't make it a big deal. Trust me."

I shook my head. "No, I want to go home."

"Tosha," Four pleaded, but I couldn't stomach looking in his direction.

"Please take me home." I grabbed my clothes and slid off his bed.

The shame was too great for me to digest, especially now. I went to the only safe space at the moment; his bathroom. I locked myself inside, using the barrier of the door as my protection for what just occurred. I fell to the ground and rested my head in my hands as reality hit me.

God, what have I done? Who have I become? Please help me be freed from this moment, I thought.

My world had turned upside down, and I had only my own actions of sin to blame.

TO BE CONTINUED...

ACKNOWLEDGMENTS

I would like to acknowledge my sister, Maryse, and our college roommate, Mayevina, for encouraging me to start writing again. Thank you for believing in me and supporting my craft. I've spent years on writing and never really thought that I could create a novel from my works. I am very proud that I am able to share my writing with all those who are reading.

I want to say thank you to all of the readers and supporters on Wattpad that encouraged me and experienced the growth of this work. I am so appreciative with all of the reviews and feedback that you all have left me. I hope that you all continue to follow the series as it expands.

FOUR'S GAME

Printed in Great Britain
by Amazon

24852089R10112